The Secret

of

Willow Patch

The Beginning

THE SECRET OF WILLOW PATCH

THE BEGINNING

BECKY AYERS

This is a work of fiction. All characters and incidents in this novel
are the products of the author's imagination.
Any similarities to people living or dead are purely coincidental.

ISBN-13: 978-1453737026 ISBN-10: 1453737022

Printed in the United States

Cover design by Tabitha Kristen

Harry Potter is a registered trademark
and a series of fantasy novels by British author J.K. Rowling

To my son Noah,

and my grandchildren

Erik, Firiona, Autumn and Jedidiah

THE BEGINNING

Chapter 1

It was a cool September morning. Not like last year when the mornings were still warm and muggy, but Tina didn't mind. She opened her bedroom window and breathed in the fresh air as she looked into the sunlit sky and watched as a flock of birds flew by. She could hear the muffled sound of her mother making breakfast through her bedroom door.

"Tina, breakfast is ready!"

Tina's stomach grumbled.

"Okay Mom, be right there!" Breakfast was always Tina's favorite meal of the day. She loved the way her mom made scrambled eggs with tiny bits of sausage in them. She flew down the stairs and jumped into her seat at the table.

"Oh my, someone is hungry this morning," her mom said with a grin. Tina breathed in the wonderful aroma of breakfast as her mom served her a healthy portion of eggs.

"Mom, have you met the family that moved in down the street yet?"

"Actually yes, I saw them taking a walk together yesterday and went out to meet them. They seem like very nice people."

"Are there any kids my age?" Tina asked hoping the kids weren't all toddlers.

"Well, let's see—if my memory serves me right there are three children. The oldest is David, he's twelve. Then there is
Sherry, she's ten. Then there is a younger one—oh yes, Cody, he's seven."

Tina nervously tapped her fork on her plate when she heard about the new neighbors. "Can I go meet them when I finish my breakfast? It sure would be nice to have some new friends to hang out with and it *is* Saturday."

Her mom glanced up at the ceiling, going over her chore list in her mind. "Sure, I guess it would be okay. Just make sure you get your bed made up before you disappear for the day." Her mom shot her one of her typical 'how could I say no to you' faces as she scrubbed the scrambled eggs out of the frying pan. Tina quickly gobbled her breakfast and slid the plate across the table to the other side so her mom could easily pick it up for washing.

"Thanks Mom. Oh, and the eggs were great as usual."

She ran to her bedroom hoping her bed was the only thing she had to tidy up before she left. Within minutes, she neatly tucked her bedspread across her bed and jumped into her favorite outfit. As she slipped her shirt over her head, she remembered the day that her mom brought it home for her.

She thought about how she had seen it in a store window one day when she and her mom had been out shopping. They were looking for a birthday present for her dad. Her mom was always good at surprising her with things she wanted. She finished pulling the shirt on and found the pair of pants that matched the beautiful violet color that she loved so much.

"My dark purple pants will look great with this shirt."

Tina had a serious fashion passion. Almost everything in her closet was some shade of purple. She took a long look in the mirror, brushed her long blonde hair, and smiled. "Yep, it looks good together alright." She grabbed her favorite pair of tennis shoes, tossed them on and ran out of her room as if her hair were on fire.

As she ran by the kitchen on her way to the front door, her mom yelled to her. "Tina, in by dark please!"

"Okay Mom," Tina replied quickly.

She ran out the door, across the yard and down the street. As she ran, she started thinking about the kids. "I wonder what they're like? They may not even be nice. What if they don't like me?"

Her steady run turned into a slow walk as she passed by all the homes between her house and the Parker home. She noticed Mrs. King had taken in her Hummingbird feeder for the winter. She remembered how she used to go to Mrs. King's house when she was very young and watch the Hummingbirds. "Good times," she thought to herself.

She walked closer to the Parkers home and her stomach started feeling a bit queasy.

"Hey! You live down the street don't you?"

Tina looked toward the Parker home and saw a girl with red hair playing with the hose on the side of the house.

3

"Hi. Yeah, I live on the opposite end of this street. My name is Tina," she said in a quiet but steady voice. She walked up to the girl and stood there shuffling her feet.

"I know, your Mom told us about you. You're twelve, right? I'm Sherry," the girl said observing how tall Tina was. "I'm ten, but almost eleven. My birthday is next month," she continued, wanting Tina to accept her as a friend even though she was younger. Sherry continued playing with the hose.

"So what are you doing?" Tina asked while watching Sherry as she sprayed the side of their house.

"I'm not doing anything really. I'm bored." She turned off the hose and looked Tina up and down.

"So, you want to go do something?"

Tina thought for a minute and came up with an idea. "We could go to my house and hang out; I have some really good Harry Potter books."

Sherry grimaced as if Tina had suggested eating broccoli. "Don't get me wrong, I like to read too. I do it a lot on my computer— but I kind of wanted to do something outside."

Tina watched as Mrs. King's car drove by. She thought to herself. 'Wish I was in that car with Mrs. King, she's fun.' She tapped her foot as she tried to think of something they could do.

"Hey Sherry, who's she?" A voice came from the upstairs window of Sherry's home.

"It's none of your business David! Leave me alone!" Sherry rolled her eyes.

"Oh, it's your little brother huh?" Tina said with a grin.

"Actually he's my big brother, but he's *so* not fun." She giggled at the thought of a boy having fun doing anything that girls like to do. "David's okay for a boy, but he's my brother."

Tina laughed as the two of them walked toward the sidewalk that ran through their quaint little neighborhood.

"So, what do you like to do for fun Tina?" Tina wasted no time telling Sherry all about her favorite hobby.

"Oh, I love to read Harry Potter books. I have all of them," Tina gestured with her hands the size of the stack of books she prized.

"That's cool. I like computers. Mom says I should work with computers when I grow up. I spend most of my free time glued to mine," Sherry chuckled.

"I don't have a computer. My parents would rather see me read books than spend all my time playing with a computer. I would like to try one someday though," said Tina, sounding a bit on the jealous side.

"You can try my computer someday. But let's do something outside today; my brothers are getting on my nerves."

"Yeah, my mom told me that you had two brothers. That must be nice."

Sherry laughed aloud. "Are you serious? Brothers are a big pain in the butt!"

Tina was amazed by Sherry's statement. "How can you say that? You don't know how lucky you are to have brothers to play with. I don't have any brothers or sisters. It's really boring at my house." Tina had a sad look on her face. "I have been wishing for a brother or sister for years, but Mom and Dad said that if they had another kid, they wouldn't be able to give me the things that they do. They said it would cost more to have another one."

Sherry nodded. "Yeah, they're right. My parents can't afford a whole lot because there are three of us. They had to save for like forever before they could buy my computer."

Tina looked at the ground. "I guess everyone has some kind of problems that they have to deal with. Oh well, let's do something. I don't want to waste this weekend."

Sherry smiled at Tina. "Yeah, let's have some fun. What is there to do around here anyway? I'm kind of used to my old neighborhood. We had a really nice park close by and a lot of stores around to look in," Sherry bragged.

"Well, we don't have any of that stuff unless you want to drive a long way to get there, but there are a lot of woods around here."

Sherry sighed. "Lead on."

They walked toward the trees in the distance, kicking stones along the way.

"Have you ever seen a deer?" Tina asked Sherry.

"No. You mean like Rudolf?" Sherry said in a sarcastic voice.

"Well, sort of. Their noses don't glow or anything, but I see them a lot in the woods. They're really pretty and sometimes you can get really close to them."

Tina picked up a rock and threw it toward the woods ahead of them.

"Can I pet one?" Sherry asked curiously.

"No, they'll run off before you get that close."

Sherry sighed again as she followed Tina up the road. The sky began to cloud up a bit as the pair entered the thick tree line at the end of the road.

"I hope it doesn't rain today. All the animals will hide if it does," Tina said. She looked up at the sky and watched the clouds float by.

"I like the rain. My friends and I used to play in the puddles after a storm in my old neighborhood. It was a lot of fun on a hot day. Don't you ever do things like that here?" Sherry questioned Tina.

"Not really, you and your brothers are the first kids to move into this neighborhood besides me. Most of the people here have lived here their entire lives and their kids have grown up and moved away."

Sherry's face looked sad. "Man, don't you get bored?"

"Yeah, sometimes I do, but most of the time I read when I don't have chores or something else to do."

The trees got thicker and thicker as they walked deeper into the woods. The sound of birds and other wild animals became louder as they walked.

"Geez, it's kind of creepy in here." Sherry stepped over old tree stumps and vines.

"Not really. I think it's relaxing and pretty. You just aren't used to it." Tina giggled. "Over there is my reading spot. I come here a lot when I get a new Harry Potter book and don't want any interruptions."

Sherry looked ahead to see it. She stared in amazement as her eyes focused on the thickest, tallest tree she had ever seen. "Wow! That's *huge!*" She noticed that at the bottom of the tree was a series of intertwined roots above ground, serving as a shelter for kids to hang out in, or even adults.

"Yeah, I love this tree. As long as I can remember, I have been coming here." She crawled up under its massive roots and motioned for Sherry to join her.

"We didn't have anything this cool in my old neighborhood." Sherry looked out from under the roots at the beautiful foliage all around her. A strong feeling of peace came over her. The girls looked at each other and laughed.

"We can *never* tell my brothers about this place," Sherry insisted.

Hence, they made a pact to keep the big tree a secret from the boys. From that day on, Sherry and Tina would be best friends.

They talked about everything from Sherry's school teachers to boys in school that she liked. Although Sherry hadn't met any of the kids at Middleton Heights yet, she still had plenty of stories from her old school to tell Tina.

She made sure she mentioned her role in the school play where she did an excellent rendition of Martha Washington and how her name was in the school newspaper. Everyone in school raved for weeks about her role making her very popular. Sherry impressed Tina with the story.

"I've never been in a play. I think I would just shrivel up and die if I had to act in front of a whole bunch of people." Tina turned bright red.

"It's not a big deal. Dad taught me to just picture everyone in the audience in their underwear. It really works. Don't *ever* look at your principle that way though. It's frightening!" Sherry let loose a deep belly laugh. Tina chuckled at the thought.

"Hey, I'm kind of hungry. Wanna go to my house and get some lunch?" Sherry asked as she held her stomach.

"Yeah, I'm kind of hungry. We've been gone quite a while."

On the way back to the Parker home, they picked some wild flowers to put in a vase for Sherry's mom.

When they walked through the door, Sherry's mom, Melinda, was sitting in the living room folding a pile of laundry she had just dried.

"Mom, this is Tina. She lives up the street. We picked you some pretty flowers to put in the dining room."

Melinda smiled and searched the bottom cabinet of the armoire for a vase.

"It's nice to meet you Tina. I'm Melinda Parker. I'm glad to see Sherry has already made a friend here." She smiled at Tina nervously. Sweat rolled down both sides of her pretty face.

"It's nice to meet you too ma'am. You have a very nice house."

Tina glanced around the room, noticing all the rather expensive Lladro figurines that covered the tables.

She remembered Mrs. King showing her a beautiful figurine at her home once. She said it was a Lladro. It was blue and white in color and very elegant looking. She thought about how much she loved one in particular that Mrs. King kept up high on a shelf. It was a little girl and a duck walking together. Tina always fancied herself a naturalist, a sort of "Dr. Doolittle". She loved animals and the outdoors.

"Those are beautiful figurines, Mrs. Parker."

"Please call me Melinda, all of the kids in our old neighborhood did."

Tina blushed. "Oh, okay Melinda. I'm sorry. People around here are very old fashioned and don't allow kids to call them by their first names. By the way, my parents are Charles and Lilly Brooks," she said as Mrs. Parker arranged the flowers in the vase.

"Yes, I remember meeting your mother the day after we moved in. She's a very nice woman."

Melinda stood up from the couch with a stack of folded clothes. "And don't worry about calling me by my first name. It makes me feel younger." Melinda wiped the sweat from her face and headed up the stairs to the kid's bedrooms.

"Your mom is very nice Sherry."

Sherry nodded. "Yeah, she's great, but she works too much," Sherry replied.

"She works too much?"

"Yeah, she has O.C.D."

"What's that?" Tina looked baffled.

"It's hard to explain but it's like an illness. She has to keep everything really clean and everything has to stay in a certain spot."

"Wow, that's an illness? I thought that was just being a mom," Tina giggled.

"Yeah well, she obsesses about the cleanliness of our house, almost to the point of exhausting herself. She's always worried that someone will see it looking messy, so she cleans all the time. But we try not to make a big deal out of it because that only makes it worse."

Tina shook her head. "Very odd, but I feel sorry for her. Can't anyone help her with it? I mean isn't there a doctor she can see for it?"

"Yeah, but it hasn't worked so far. Look, it's no big deal." Sherry looked as if they were talking about the "D" she got in math class.

Tina looked embarrassed for asking too many questions about Melinda. "Oh, I didn't mean anything by that, I was just..." Tina tried to take back what she asked.

"Hey, let's go in my room after we get some sandwiches. I can show you my computer." The girls went to the kitchen and made a few ham sandwiches then ran upstairs to Sherry's room.

When they reached the top of the stairs, they ran into little Cody.

"What do you want Cody?" Sherry nervously tapped her foot.

"Who's that?" he asked while fiddling with a small toy truck.

"This is Tina, now go away, we're busy!"

Sherry grabbed Tina's arm and pulled her toward her bedroom door. Tina turned to Cody.

"Nice meeting you Cody."

11

As Tina entered Sherry's room, she heard music playing. "Hey, you have a stereo in your room?" Tina asked.

"Yeah, my dad's friend bought a new stereo and said I could have his old one. It works pretty well," she said as she turned the music off. "Come here, I want to show you my computer."

Tina walked across the room toward the window where a small desk was set up with a computer on it. "Wow, this is pretty awesome."

"I love my computer. I don't know what I would do without it." Sherry turned it on and showed Tina what she could do with it. "I can do all sorts of stuff on here. I can keep a diary that my brothers can't get into, I can play games, study for my classes and best of all I can paint and draw. I have a ton of things that I made and saved on here. Want to try?"

Tina looked at the computer as if it were a monster with three heads. "I don't know. I've never used one before. I might mess it up."

Sherry laughed. "You won't mess it up! It's okay, try it." Sherry urged Tina.

Tina grabbed a hold of the mouse and started moving it around on the mouse pad making swirls and patterns.

"Whoa, this is pretty cool!" She giggled and bounced in the chair as she turned her elementary lines into actual pictures.

"When you're done, you can save the picture, and I can print it out for you," Sherry told her as she leaned over Tina.

"Okay, I'm done."

Sherry clicked a couple buttons and began printing the picture.

"This is so cool Sherry. You're lucky to have a computer."

Sherry smiled as she handed the picture to Tina. "I know. It's pretty awesome."

Tina took the picture, folded it up and put it in her pocket. "My mom is going to love this picture," Tina said with a prideful smile.

"I make a lot of drawings, but most of them I just keep on my computer," Sherry said, as she went through the pictures she had stored on her computer.

"Sherry!" Tina jumped when she heard a loud bang at the door. "Sherry! Are you in there?"

"Aw geez, it's my dorky brother," she said with a sigh. "What the heck does he want?" She walked to her door and opened it just a bit, making sure her foot was behind the door to keep him from entering. "What do you want David?"

"What are you doing in there? Is that girl from down the street here?"

"Yes, and her name is Tina. Now go away nosey!"

"I need to come in; I think I left my camera in there the other day." Sherry grew impatient. "No! Go *away*," she said with a louder and sterner voice.

"But I need that camera! Let me in!" He pushed hard on the door.

"Mom, would you tell David to leave us alone!"

Tina sat and watched the feud between brother and sister and wondered what it felt like.

Melinda rushed up the stairs to settle the argument. "What on earth is going on up here?" she said, sounding out of breath.

"Mom, Tina and I are trying to talk and David won't leave us alone!"

"But she has my camera in there and won't give it back!"

Melinda stifled the kids with a resounding *"Enough!"*

Sherry and David stood there in the hallway with looks of contempt on their faces.

"Sherry, do you have David's camera?"

"No Mom, he's just saying that so he can get into my bedroom and bug us!"

"You're such a liar Sherry! You know you have it!"

"Do *not!*"

"I said that's enough and I mean it!" Melinda stomped her foot as she tried to control the situation. "Okay Sherry, back in your room. David, go outside or in your room or—something. We'll find your camera later." She turned and walked back downstairs.

David walked toward his bedroom as Sherry went back into hers and shut the door.

"Sheesh! See what I mean? Brothers are such a pain!"

Tina tried not to show her amusement toward the whole thing and turned away from Sherry to hide her smile.

"Let's go back to the tree so we can talk without my brothers bothering us."

"Okay. I don't have to be home until right before it gets dark."

"Cool, we have lots of time, then."

On their way, they stopped in the kitchen to grab a bag full of cookies for the walk. Melinda was washing lunch dishes.

"Where are you girls off to now?" Sherry's mother asked of them politely.

"We're going to our secret spot. We went there earlier. It's really pretty." Sherry zipped the bag shut.

"Okay, well—don't be out too late please. Your dad says there are wild animals around here and I don't want you running into any of them."

Tina giggled.

"Okay, Mom, see ya later."

"Bye Mrs.—I mean, Melinda," Tina said blushing.

"Oh man, you're never going to get used to that are ya?" asked Sherry as she opened the front door to leave. "Come on, let's get out of here."

As they walked through Sherry's front yard, Tina thought about how nice and refreshing it was to hear them arguing. Surely, they didn't fight all the time, there had to be some times when they got along and had fun together.

"Sherry, do you and David fight a lot?"

"Nah, not too much. I mean, we get on each other's nerves sometimes. We love each other, but don't ever quote me." She snorted as she laughed.

"Do you get along with Cody too?"

"Yeah, I guess. He's my little brother and I try to help him with things, but sometimes he can be annoying. I remember when he was still wearing diapers; he was a cute little booger. I used to sing songs and read stories to him. It was a lot of fun."

"You're so lucky Sherry." Tina stared at the ground as they walked.

"I wouldn't call it luck, but I guess it is nice to have brothers. I just wish I had a sister."

They closed in on the woods. The breeze cut through the tall trees making an eerie sound that was familiar only to Tina.

"Think of it this way Sherry, if something gets broken in your house, your parents don't automatically blame you," Tina said, laughing.

"That's very true." Sherry cracked a devious smile.

They entered the woods once again. The sun was trying to break through the clouds that hung in the sky most of that morning. The silence of the woods was not like the silence of anywhere else in the world. It was filled with the peaceful sounds of nature.

Sherry made a beeline for the beauty of the secret spot. "Hurry up Tina," she yelled as she jumped over the stumps and vines that she crossed earlier that day. The shade of the huge tree was inviting. Sherry plopped herself down at the foot of the tree. "Man, this is beautiful!"

Tina caught up to Sherry. "I know. There's nowhere else on this earth I would rather be. And you are the *only* other person that knows about it," said Tina.

They sat down together and looked up at the tree tops and imagined how beautiful a view it must be from way up there.

"Man, I wish I had a digital camera like David," said Sherry. "I'd love to take some pictures out here to use as backgrounds on my computer. Tina?"

"Yes?" she replied.

"Do you ever have dreams that you could fly?"

Tina responded quickly. "All the time. I love those dreams."

Sherry stared at the sky through the trees. "Sometimes they seem so real, and then I wake up and realize it was just a dream and I get sad."

"I know. That happens to me too."

They stared at the sky silently. The sun broke away most of the clouds, leaving only a few wisps that resembled shreds of cotton.

"Aw, isn't that so cute!"

The girls jumped up, shocked. They looked around to find where the voice was coming from.

"David?" Sherry asked. They heard a rustling of branches behind a nearby tree. "David? That's not funny!" Then they heard laughing. "David! Get out of here! This is *our* secret spot! No *boys* allowed!" As they stood up to look for him, he jumped out from behind the tree.

"*Aha*! So *this* is where you guys went earlier today."

"It's none of your business David! Go home!" Sherry stomped her feet toward David.

"Why? What are you guys doing out here anyway?" David pulled his camera out of his pocket and started taking pictures of his sister's tirade. Tina giggled as she watched them get into it again.

"Stop taking pictures of me and go home! And I'm telling Mom that you had your camera the whole time! You just wanted to be nosey!" Sherry responded in a huff.

"Aw, let him stay Sherry. He won't hurt anything," Tina said with a smile.

"Are you serious? He's my brother!" Sherry looked at Tina as if she had lost her mind.

"Sure, it'll be fun." Sherry shrugged her shoulders as she heard more noise from behind the tree.

"What the…?" Sherry said with a puzzled look on her face.

Tina looked in the direction that Sherry was looking. Out from behind the tree popped Cody.

David snickered. "Oh yeah, I brought Cody with me."

"For crying out loud David!" Sherry stomped in circles.

"It's okay Sherry; I think your brothers are cool. Besides, the more the merrier, right?"

Sherry looked at Tina. "Uhm, hello? These are my stupid brothers. I don't see any merriness happening with them around!"

Tina laughed. "Sherry, you crack me up."

David looked at the shelter area at the bottom of the tree and snapped some pictures of it. "Wow, look at this Code!"

Cody walked over to the tree and crawled under the roots. "Awesome!" David joined his brother.

"Great! Now they'll never leave!" Sherry plopped down onto the dirt. "Before you know it they'll have stupid fort flags all over this tree and a sign that says 'No Girls Allowed!'"

Tina walked over to David and Cody. "You can come here, but please don't try to turn it into a fort. This place is special to me. Don't ask me why, I just know I have been coming here for years and I don't want it ruined." She smiled gently at the boys. David smiled back at Tina.

"Yeah, we wouldn't ever do that anyway. This is a cool tree; it deserves to be left alone."

Sherry rolled her eyes in disbelief. "Like *you* care."

"I do Sherry. When I first saw this tree, before you guys saw me, I don't know— it made me feel different."

Tina listened intently to what David was saying. "You feel it too?" Tina thought it was just her.

"Yeah, I mean, it makes me feel kind of—I don't know. Peaceful."

Sherry perked up. "You guys too?"

Tina looked at Sherry. "What do you mean, Sherry?"

"I feel the same way you and David feel, kind of peaceful, but not the average peaceful you feel when you are in a park or something. This is totally different."

"I feel it too," Cody responded to the conversation.

They stood around looking at each other as if they had found lost treasure.

Tina spoke like she was keeping a secret. "All these years that I have been coming here I thought it was just me. I thought everyone else would just see it as any other tree. This is weird guys. I wonder if something cool happened here a long time ago or something."

They contemplated the possibilities of why they would all have such a strange feeling about that tree, just that one tree.

"Guys, we have to keep this place a secret from everyone else. Other people might come around here if they think there is something special about this tree. Let's make a pact to keep it a secret until we find out more," David said.

"Uhm hello? Tina and I already made a pact!" blurted Sherry. "But, since you've both already been here and seen how cool it is, I guess we'll add you to the pact too." She rolled her eyes at David.

They all shook hands on it and began to walk back home. The group walked through the woods toward the exit, thinking about the tree, wondering why and how this could be happening. It's just a tree right? Who knows?

They made it back to the Parker home and sat at the kitchen table while having some cold drinks.

Melinda walked in. "That was a quick day for you kids," she said.

The kids sat there looking at each other as if to say, 'Don't say a thing'.

"So, where did you go?"

Tina took it upon herself to do the answering. "I just took them to a place in the woods that I thought was pretty cool. We played tag for a while. That's all."

Melinda grabbed her broom and started sweeping up dirt that the kids dragged in on their shoes. "I see, and you brought me back a souvenir." Cody chuckled. "David, you need to clean your room. I noticed you left some clothes on the floor and didn't close your drawers."

"I know Mom. I'll go do it now." He put his drink on the table and stumbled up the stairs, mumbling the whole way.

"Mom, do you mind if we go back with Tina again tonight after dinner?" Sherry asked as she sloshed her drink in circles inside the glass.

"Won't it be kind of late after dinner?" Melinda answered.

"No ma'am, it doesn't get dark until about ten P.M. around here this time of the year."

Melinda shook her head. "Oh that's right, I forgot about that. We've only been here a few days and I guess it's going to take me some time to get used to that." She continued sweeping. "I suppose it would be okay but you might want to clear it with your dad when he gets home."

Sherry nodded."I'm going to go take a bath Tina, I'll see you later okay?"

Tina stood up. "Okay, come over to my house when you're done eating dinner."

"Sure, you live in the brown house with the dog house in the front yard right?"

Tina grinned. "It's not really a dog house. My parents would never let me have a dog. They say they're too messy. That's a cover for our well."

Sherry raised an eyebrow. "Uhm, okay—whatever. I'll come down as soon as I finish."

Tina nodded and started home.

Chapter 2

Tina noticed as she walked, that she could hear a sound that she had never heard before. It was like the wind that she always heard, but this time it was creepy. It almost sounded like a whisper. She ignored the odd feeling the sound gave her and continued on her way home. When she approached her house, her father drove up.

"Hey you! What are you up to?"

"Hi Daddy. I just met our new neighbors. They're really nice."

He turned the car off and got out. "That's nice Honey. Any kids your age?"

She gave her dad a hug. "Yeah, David is my age and Sherry is ten, but she's really cool, and they have a seven year-old brother. His name is Cody."

Her father walked toward the house and opened the door. "Lilly! I'm home." He walked into the kitchen and grabbed a cold drink.

"So where did you go today?" Tina tried to make conversation with her dad.

"Oh, I met some fellow bankers at the golf course. I didn't play very well today though." He hung his head in mock shame.

The Beginning

"Oh Daddy, you're the best golfer I know." Tina smiled at her father lovingly.

"Thank you honey, but I'm the only golfer you know." He chuckled and walked around the house looking for Lilly.

"Charles, I'm in here!" He walked toward their bedroom.

"There you are!" He smiled as he walked over to Lilly who was reading a book.

"So how did your golfing go today honey," she asked as she flipped through the pages.

"Oh, no worse than the last time I played. No better either."

Tina sat on her parent's bed and listened in.

"Oh, before I forget, the next time you're in town, could you pick up some rosin for me? I'm just about out and can't play in the next concert without it."

"Of course. I can't bear the thought of not hearing you practice at night before I go to sleep. It relaxes me and makes the stresses of my day just fade away." Lilly smiled at Charles.

"Mom?" Tina interrupted her parent's conversation. "What is rosin for?"

Her father answered. "That's what your mother puts on her bow when she plays her cello. Without that, the bow would just slide across the strings and wouldn't make a sound. The rosin is a dry but sticky substance that causes the bow to rub the strings, causing a vibration and sound."

Tina nodded. "Oh I get it, sort of like when I use my wet finger to make music with glasses full of water?"

23

Her mother giggled. "Well not exactly, but we'll go with that idea for now."

Tina stood up and walked toward her parent's door. "What's for dinner tonight?"

Lilly closed her book and answered Tina. "I think I'll make a couple frozen pizzas tonight. Sound good to you?"

Tina grinned from ear to ear. "Awesome!"

She darted out of the doorway and ran to her room. She flopped on her bed and gazed up at a Harry Potter poster she had pinned to her ceiling.

"I wish I was artistic," she said as she looked at the fine details of the poster. She walked over to her desk and dug around for a clean sheet of paper and some colored pencils. She began to draw the tree and its surroundings. Tina wasn't the best of artists; in fact her drawings came out rather juvenile looking. Still this one had something that none of the others had, even better than the one she did on Sherry's computer earlier that day. The shading was perfect, and the tree almost had a 3-D look to it. It was almost startling how well it came out.

She could smell the pizza cooking as she drew the scenery around the tree. Her stomach rumbled loudly. "I am so hungry. Mom! How long 'til the pizza is done?"

She could faintly hear her mom say 'in a minute'. She continued drawing, adding foliage until it was finished. It was amazing. It looked as if she had taken a picture with a camera, but still she knew she had just drawn the picture herself. 'I don't understand' she thought to herself. 'How on earth did I draw it that well?'

"Dinner!" Tina's mom yelled from downstairs.

Tina stood up and glanced at the door then glanced back at the picture. "Unbelievable." She shook her head and went downstairs to eat dinner.

The smell of the pizza as she walked toward the kitchen was wonderful. It wasn't her mom's special scrambled eggs, but it was a close second place for favorite foods. She sat at the table and grabbed a piece. "Mom, this is great!"

Lilly smiled. "Well, it's not as good as take out, but we're too far away from town. By the time we got it back here it would be rather cold and rubbery."

Charles grinned at Lilly. "Yeah, there's a great pizza place in town, I get a slice to go on occasion during the week, but we're just too far away. Maybe we'll all go someday and get some."

"That would be nice dad, thanks." Tina changed the subject. "Uhm, Mom? Would it be okay for me to go back to Sherry's house after dinner?"

"It's okay with me as long as your father doesn't mind." Tina turned to her dad. "Daddy?"

He reached for another slice of pizza. "Sure, but you get back here before dark, you know the rules."

"Okay Daddy, thanks." She finished her last bite of pizza and headed up to her room to get the picture she drew before dinner.

"Man, I still can't believe this." She ran out the front door and headed to Sherry's house. She approached the house and noticed a car in the driveway that wasn't there before. She walked up and knocked on the door. She heard David yelling.

"I'll get it!" The door flew open. "Oh, hey Tina. Sherry is almost done eating. She's slow." He laughed.

"That's okay, I'll wait out here."

"Nah, you can come in and wait." She went inside and heard Sherry talking with her dad.

"David was being a jerk today, Dad. He said I took his camera and I really didn't."

Tina heard Sherry's father clear his throat. "Your mom told me about it. I think David has forgotten about the whole camera thing, don't you?" Sherry was hoping David would be in trouble, but found out that before it had started, it had ended.

Sherry walked out of the kitchen with a frown on her face.

"What's wrong Sherry," Tina asked.

"Nothing. It's just my dad is letting David slide on the whole camera thing that happened today. I'm so tired of him getting his way." She motioned for Tina to follow her to her bedroom.

"Sherry, not to change the subject or anything, but I need to talk to you about something that happened."

Sherry opened her bedroom door and turned the stereo on. "What's up?" Sherry asked in a rather cold tone.

Tina pulled the picture of the tree out of her pocket. The picture she made on Sherry's computer fell to the floor. "When I went home earlier, I made this picture. Look at it." She handed it to Sherry and bent over to pick up the picture she made of the swirls and patterns.

"Okay, where did you get this?" Sherry questioned Tina in a sarcastic tone.

The Beginning

"I didn't *get* it anywhere Sherry, I drew this myself!"

Sherry looked disturbed. "But that's impossible! It looks like a photograph! I bet David gave this to you after he took pictures of the tree to pull a prank on me, right? Nobody could have drawn this Tina!" Sherry tossed the picture on her bed and turned her back to Tina. "I can't believe that you would actually expect me to believe this. I thought we were friends." Sherry lowered her head in disappointment.

Tina unfolded the picture that Sherry printed out for her earlier. "What?" Tina said in a shocked voice.

Sherry turned to look at Tina. Tina stared at the picture that Sherry printed for her earlier, not wanting to believe that it could really be the same picture.

"What's wrong," Sherry asked insensitively.

Tina handed the printed picture to Sherry; her hand was shaking.

Sherry looked at the picture. "What's going on here? Where did you get this? Is this some sort of joke? 'Cuz if it is, it's not funny."

Tina looked up to the ceiling as if she was clueless as well. "No it's not a joke Sherry. That's the picture that I drew on your computer! You printed it out for me."

Sherry looked at the picture closer.

"It *is* your picture! I can see the lines of it in the background, but there's a photo of the tree over top of it!"

Tina nodded. "It's been in my pocket all day."

Sherry flipped the picture over and inspected the back of it. "And it's just like the one you drew at home, same angle of the tree and everything."

27

"Why is this happening?" Sherry asked Tina, sounding beyond freaked out. Tina walked to the window and looked out.

"Sherry, there's something else I need to tell you."

Sherry walked over to Tina with a look of concern.

"When I was walking home today, I heard something strange." She picked at her fingernails.

"What was it Tina?"

"It was the wind, but it sounded different, like a voice whispering to me." She looked at Sherry wondering if she would think she was crazy.

"A voice? What kind of voice? What did it say?"

Sherry stood there waiting for an answer from Tina, but Tina wasn't comfortable about telling Sherry. Sherry came from a totally different kind of life than Tina, and Tina didn't want her to think she was crazy. She needed her friendship. She had been alone with nobody but adults to talk to, her whole life. But Sherry didn't know that because she wasn't aware that Tina was homeschooled, so she didn't even see children on weekdays. Sherry was very important to Tina and she was willing to do whatever she had to do to keep her as a friend.

"Cody! How many times has Mom said to stay on the sidewalk?" David yanked his brother back onto the sidewalk as they walked down toward the woods. "I want to go look at that tree again. There's something about it—I don't know what it is, but I just need to go there again."

Cody tried to keep up with David as he picked up the pace.

"David?"

"What, squirt?"

"Maybe we should wait for the girls."

David walked even faster as if being pulled toward the woods.

"David?" Cody started running slowly to keep up with David. "David!"

"What?"

Cody stopped in his tracks. "I said maybe we should wait for the girls."

David smiled at his brother. "Why? I just want to take a quick look; it won't hurt anything to go there for just a second."

Cody shrugged his shoulders. "Yeah, I guess it's okay."

David continued the pace drawing nearer to the tree line. Cody was a bit concerned about David's behavior, but followed his brother anyway. They felt a cool breeze as they entered the woods. David came to a halt like he had just run into an invisible wall.

"What's wrong David?" David stared straight ahead, his eyes glazed over. "David? David what's wrong?"

David turned to Cody. "Did you hear that?" He turned his ear toward the tree.

"Hear what?" Cody asked with a look of confusion on his face.

"That whispering sound. You didn't hear that?"

Cody stood in silence and listened. "Nope. What did it sound like?"

David got aggravated at his little brother. "It *sounded* like a whisper!"

Cody stepped back. "I didn't hear it, sorry."

David looked ahead of them. "But I could've sworn..." He shook his head and kept walking.

Cody was worried more than ever about his brother's odd behavior."Maybe it was just the wind going through the leaves. Remember when we went camping with dad that time and the sound of the wind scared me? You told me that it was just the wind going through the leaves and branches. You said I shouldn't let it scare me."

David stopped in his tracks. "Look Code, I just said that to make you feel better 'cuz it was your first time camping. I have no idea what causes the wind to make weird sounds, all I know is that what I just heard wasn't a "normal" wind sound. There was whispering."

Cody listened again, but heard nothing. They continued walking to the tree, confused and afraid.

Chapter 3

Sherry walked to her bed and sat down. "So you're saying that you heard a whisper, for sure, but you have no clue what it was saying?" Tina nodded and walked over to Sherry.

"I guess it does sound a bit crazy, but I swear, it really happened. Please don't think I'm nuts or anything. I'm only telling you this—well, because you're the only friend I have. It's easier to tell a friend than a parent when it comes to weird stuff like this."

Sherry nodded. "Yeah, I understand that. Well, my dad isn't so hard to talk to about weird stuff. He's a writer and has a very open mind. My mom on the other hand wouldn't want to hear about it. She gets freaked out easily. She won't even watch any scary movies with us." She chuckled.

Tina cracked a grin. "Well, I just don't want to lose you as a friend, that's all. I mean, we just met each other today, ya know?"

Sherry leaned over and gave Tina a hug. "Yeah, it is kind of nice. Even though we really don't have a lot in common, we have a lot of fun together. You can be the sister I never got." Sherry shot a smile at Tina.

Tina smiled back. "Yeah, sisters."

David and Cody approached the tree. "I can't get over how cool this tree is," David said to Cody as he snapped a few more pictures of it. They looked closely at the tree.

"Hey David, look what I found."

David looked at Cody. "What?"

"Look at the tree here." David leaned toward the heavy trunk of the tree. He mumbled. "C.B. and L.L." He rubbed his fingers across the engraving on the tree.

"What does that mean David?"

"It means that two people we here once and they were in love." Cody nodded his head.

"And what does this one mean?" He pointed to another spot on the tree.

David read the words. "We swear our silence." Cody waited to hear an explanation.

"Well, someone swore to never tell about something, but I don't know what. Strange." David took pictures of the carvings as they stood in deep thought. "I'll dump the pictures on dad's computer when we get home." The breeze picked up again. David jumped away from the tree. "Did you hear it that time?"

Cody looked astonished. "Yeah, I heard that. What was it?"

David listened closely to hear it again. "What did it sound like to you Code?"

Cody put his finger to his chin. "It kind of sounded like "pillow catch" to me."

David looked at Cody like he had just ruined the punch line of a joke. "Pillow catch, Code? What the heck is that? You suppose the tree wants to have a pillow fight? Come on!"

Cody shrugged his shoulders.

David turned his camera on and switched it to video so he could record the sound, but they didn't hear it again.

"Maybe we should go back home. The girls are probably wondering where we are."

They started on their way back out of the woods.

"Maybe we should walk backward so nothing can sneak up behind us," Cody said in a joking way.

"Cut it out, squirt! You're giving me the creeps!"

They tried to ignore the feeling of wanting to run until they reached the tree lined exit.

"Okay, let's go talk to the girls." They ran to their house where they met up with Sherry and Tina.

"So what should we do?" Sherry asked Tina who was studying the picture that she drew at home.

"I'm not sure. Maybe we should go to the tree again."

"I don't know Tina; I'm starting to think that place is weird." Tina paced the floor. "All these years, I have been going there to read my books since I was old enough to read. I just don't understand it. Why is this happening *now*?" She brushed her blonde hair out of her eyes.

David swung Sherry's door open. "Sherry! We gotta talk!" He shut the door and walked over to sit on her bed. "There's some very strange stuff going on in the woods, Cody and I were just in there."

Sherry stood up. "Why did you go without us?"

"Sherry, you don't understand! Something's not right, I mean, the whispering I heard."

Tina stood up. "Whispering? You heard whispering?" she asked David, sounding alarmed.

"What did it say? David, you have to tell us!" Sherry asked, practically yelling.

"We're not really sure, but it sounded sort of like…"

"Pillow catch!" Cody blurted out.

Sherry sat back down on the bed. "For crying out loud Cody! Pillow catch?" She laughed.

"Wait, maybe you heard it wrong. I heard whispering, too, when I was going home earlier today, but I couldn't understand it. Maybe you just didn't understand it, like me," Tina said trying to calm them all down.

David looked embarrassed. "I don't know, it happened so quickly and it was so quiet, it was really hard to tell. I tried to record it with my digital camera, but it didn't do it once I turned it on." David sounded aggravated. "But I have pictures on my camera that I need to dump. I can either use your computer or Dad's." David said to Sherry.

"My computer is almost out of space. You better put them on Dad's computer. His has a lot of room left," Sherry insisted.

David went to his parent's room, hooked his camera up and loaded the pictures onto his father's computer. David was confused. Not one of the pictures that he took of the carvings showed the words. Almost as if they really weren't on the tree. "What the heck is going on? I know I got at least one good shot of the carvings." David closed the picture folder and went back to Sherry's room.

Chapter 4

"I wonder where Tina is. I hope she remembers to get back home before dark," said Charles, as he thumbed through bills.

"I'm sure she'll be back on time," said Lilly.

Charles glanced at Lilly over his glasses. "She has friends now Lilly. Kids do silly things and lose track of time when they are around friends."

Lilly walked over and rubbed Charles' shoulders in a calming way. "She'll be okay honey. She's never let us down before. Besides, she's getting a bit old for that 'be in before dark' rule since we don't live in the city."

Charles stood up from his chair and removed his glasses. "We made a promise to each other before she was born that if we moved back here, she would never be allowed out after dark. Remember?" He put his glasses back on.

"Yes. I know dear, but someday she will be too old for that rule. How are we going to explain to her when she's fifteen or sixteen that she still has to be in the house before dark?"

"Then I guess we'll have to tell her, but until then...in by dark," Charles replied.

Lilly quietly walked out of the room. Charles continued going through the bills.

∾⭒⭒

Sherry, Tina, David and Cody walked down the stairs and told Melinda that they were going back out.

"Mom? Dad? Hello?" Sherry bellowed through the house. The four of them walked together from room to room looking for Melinda and Ken.

"Ken, I can't take anymore. I'm frightened." The kids stood outside their parents door listening.

"Honey, come on. I'm sure it's just their imaginations getting away with them. You know how kids are," Ken tried to calm his wife.

Sherry looked at David like he had the answer to what they were talking about.

"They said something about a whisper; they heard whispering for crying out loud! David, Tina and Cody all heard it!"

Sherry pushed the door open slightly. She watched her father give her mother a hug.

"Melinda, please don't let this bother you. You know how you have a tendency to worry too much. You'll make yourself sick again. Really, I'm sure it's nothing more than kids trying to scare each other."

Melinda stood up and Sherry noticed the tears rolling down her mother's face.

Sherry whispered to David. "She must have been standing outside our door when we were talking about the tree."

David's head dropped. "Man, we should've gone outside to talk about it."

Sherry and Tina nodded. They walked away from the door feeling rather foolish.

"I'll leave a note on the fridge so they know where we are," explained Sherry. She scribbled a quick note and used her favorite USB magnet to attach it to the front of the refrigerator. The four walked out the front door quietly.

"David," Cody said the minute they got out the door. David looked at him.

"Are ya gonna to tell them about the words on the tree?" Sherry and Tina stopped walking.

"Words? There are words on the tree?" Sherry asked, hoping she heard him wrong.

"Yeah, Code and I saw something written on the tree when we went there a while ago. I took pictures, but when I dumped the camera on Dads computer, the words weren't on the tree."

He started walking in the direction of the woods.

"What did it say on the tree David?" Tina inquired looking a bit curious.

"Well, in one spot it just had initials, but in another spot it said 'We swear our silence'."

"I have *never* seen any initials or writing of any kind on that tree. I've been going there since I was really young," said Tina, sounding confused.

"Silence? About what?" Sherry asked. She continued walking. "Man, this just keeps getting weirder and weirder."

"Maybe the initials have something to do with the whispering," said Tina.

"I don't know. The initials were in a totally different spot on the tree," David responded. They made it to the tree line and stopped for a minute.

"Maybe Cody should go back home," Sherry said to David.

"I think he should go with us. Besides, it's not going to be dark for another four hours," David replied.

Sherry looked at her watch and nodded. They walked toward the tree. As they walked through the thick trees, getting closer and closer to Tina's reading spot, they noticed the wind picking up. Branches on trees started bending and bobbing around, making the once quiet woods a bit on the noisy side.

"Geez, why is it only windy when we come here?" Sherry asked Tina.

"I don't know, but it didn't always do this."

They finally reached the tree. David pointed to the area on the tree where the writing was. Sherry and Tina walked over to the tree and looked for the writing that David pointed to.

"Where is it David?" Tina asked him.

"It's right there. Don't you see it?"

Tina and Sherry looked all around the tree and saw no trace of writing of any kind. David walked closer to the tree to show the girls where it was.

"But, it was right here and the other one was over there. What happened to it?" Sherry and Tina looked at David for an explanation.

"Cody, you saw it too. Tell them!"

"Yeah, I saw it too Sherry," Cody said, shuffling his feet in the dirt around the tree. They all sat down near the roots.

The Beginning

"How could something that was engraved just disappear like that?" David picked up piles of dirt and threw it down in anger.

"Look, maybe you just thought you saw letters. Maybe it was just a combination of the grain in the bark and the sun shining through the trees," Tina said gently, knowing that David was on the edge.

"Yeah, and maybe you didn't hear the wind whispering today either," David said in a huff.

"Hey, David! Tina was just trying to make sense of this; you don't have to bite her head off!" said Sherry, defending her new best friend. David's face turned bright red with embarrassment.

"Sorry Tina, but I just don't get it. It was there, I swear it was!" David calmed down.

Tina smiled at David. "It's okay, I understand."

"So, what do we do now?" David asked.

"I'm not sure," said Tina. "Didn't you say there were initials? What were they?" Sherry tried to keep her cool. David tried to remember what he saw on the tree earlier.

"Uhm, I think it was C.D. and L.L. or something like that."

Sherry looked confused. "Well, doesn't sound familiar to me, how about you guys?" Sherry looked at David, Cody and Tina.

"No clue," Cody replied.

"What about you Tina?" David asked. "I don't know, could be anyone."

The breeze kicked up again.

"Wait, quiet!" David yelled as he turned his ear toward the tree. "Listen!"

Tina, Sherry and Cody all hushed and listened to the wind. Branches banged together and leaves rustled, the breeze turned cool again. Behind all the noise from the trees, a faint sound was heard.

"…iiiiilllllooowww…aaaaattttcccchhhh."

David jumped to his feet. "I *know* you had to hear *that!*" Sherry and Tina looked at each other in disbelief.

"I heard it!" said Sherry, nodding her head. Cody piped up. "I heard it too!"

Tina nodded her head. "Yes, I heard it too, but I could actually hear words that time."

She looked at the tree wondering what the story was with it and why this was happening then, of all times. They all sat together by the tree looking stunned. The sun began to fade into the trees and the temperature started to drop. Nighttime was on its way.

Chapter 5

Melinda nervously put away the dinner dishes that she had left to dry earlier. Her hands were shaking. She dropped a plate on her foot and yelled in pain. "Ken! Come here quick!" Ken ran into the kitchen and saw Melinda standing near the counter, her left foot was bleeding.

"Melinda! What happened?" He helped her to the kitchen chair and inspected her foot.

"I dropped a plate on it. I'm so clumsy!" She trembled all over from the pain. Sweat rolled down her face blending in with her tears.

"It's cut pretty badly. I think I'm going to have to take you to the hospital for stitches." Melinda pulled her foot away from Ken.

"No hospital! I hate those places!" she said defiantly.

"But honey, this will just keep bleeding and bleeding until it's stitched up."

"No hospital Ken! You know how I feel about hospitals." Ken looked at her foot again.

"Okay, then maybe I can wrap some bandages around it until you think about it for a while, but you have to promise me you'll stay off of it." Ken ran to their

bathroom to look for the gauze bandages they had when
Sherry fell off the swing set when she was nine. Melinda
tried to reach her broom to sweep up the glass while she
sat in the chair, but she couldn't reach it. Ken returned
with the gauze.

"Now I won't have you trying to clean when your foot
is messed up like this. Just sit still and let me wrap it up."
He took the bandages and wrapped them around
Melinda's foot several times, hoping to stop the blood flow.

"I can't believe how clumsy I am." Melinda said
again as he tended to her. "Now the floor is a mess and
the kids will be home soon."

"Don't worry about the floor. I'll clean it up. You
just relax." Ken said in a comforting tone. He picked her
up and carried her to the couch where she laid down
while he cleaned up the glass.

❧

"David?" Sherry said with a shaky voice.
"Yeah?"
"Something's wrong." Sherry urged.
"What do you mean?"
"I don't know; something feels bad." Sherry stepped
away from the tree.
"You think we should leave?" David questioned.
Tina glanced at the tree. "Why? It's not the tree. At
least I don't think it is," Tina said.
Sherry looked at David. "No David, something is
wrong at home, I don't know how I know it, but I do."
Sherry turned and started walking home.

The Beginning

"Cody, come on. We have to go home!"

Sherry started running as fast as she could. Tina, David and Cody followed.

"Hurry!" she yelled to the others. "We have to hurry!"

They ran nonstop all the way to the front door of their house. Sherry opened the door to see her mom lying on the couch, blood had soaked the cushion.

"Mom, what happened?" Sherry yelled at the sight of the blood.

"Shhhh! She's okay for now. She's sleeping but she really needs to get to a hospital for stitches," said her father in a calm voice.

David looked at her foot. "But how did this happen?"

Ken wiped the sweat from Melinda's forehead with a towel. "She dropped a plate on her foot when she was putting the dinner dishes away."

Cody knelt next to his mom and cried silently.

"She'll be okay Code; people have gotten hurt a lot worse than this and were fine," said David. He smiled at Cody.

Tina looked at Sherry, David and Cody with sadness. "I'm so sorry this happened to your mom. Maybe my parents can help in some way?"

Ken sat down in his favorite chair. "I appreciate the thought Tina, but Melinda has a fear of hospitals and it's not easy to get her to go to one, even when she's badly hurt." Tina nodded.

"I understand Mr. Parker."

43

"Please, call me Ken."

Sherry looked at Tina and smiled.

"Oh, okay—Ken. So how are you going to get her to the hospital for stitches then?"

Ken watched Melinda as she slept. "I'll talk to her about it in a while. Right now, she needs to rest. She's exhausted, as she is everyday about this time. This just put her over the edge." He stood up and walked toward the bathroom.

"Guys, let's go up to my room," Sherry said as she headed towards the stairs. "We need to talk."

Tina glanced at the old ornate clock in the Parkers living room as she walked up the stairs. "Getting late," she thought to herself. They went into Sherry's room and shut the door.

"Sherry, I'm going to have to go home soon. I have a curfew."

Sherry sat on her bed and looked at the picture of the tree again. "I know, before dark. Same rule we have here." She picked up the printed picture and compared it to the drawing. "This is so odd."

David looked at the pictures for the first time. "Why didn't you guys tell us about the pictures?"

Sherry and Tina looked at one another.

"I guess cuz we didn't understand what was going on and didn't want to scare you," Tina replied.

David looked closely at the pictures. "Where did they come from?"

Tina explained. "One is a picture I did on Sherry's computer and she printed it out. The other one is a

44

drawing I made at my house. The problem is that the printed one has a photo over top of it now and the one I drew at home looks like I took a picture of the tree with a camera."

David examined them, intent on finding an answer. "But they look like the same picture, except the one you printed has some lines and stuff in the background."

Cody looked at the pictures and shrugged his shoulders. "How could two pictures made two different ways come out looking exactly alike?"

Tina looked at the multicolored clock on Sherry's desk. "Guys, I hate to do this, but I better get home before my parents freak out. We can talk about this again tomorrow. Maybe things will look different then." She gave Sherry a hug and waved goodbye to all of them. "I hope your mom goes to the hospital tonight." She smiled at them as she walked out of the bedroom.

Tina walked out the front door of the Parker home and headed home. She saw that the sun was almost gone and the chill of the night air made her shiver as she walked along the sidewalk. She looked ahead at her house. The inside lights were on as well as the porch light. 'Well, that can't be good,' she thought to herself. "They've never had to turn the porch light on for me."

As she entered the house, she saw that her mother was a bit irritated at the hour she came in.

"Mom, I'm sorry."

Lilly stood up from her chair. "You really pushed us tonight young lady. I thought it was totally clear that you were to be in before dark; *well* before dark."

Tina hung her head while her mother scolded her.

"But Mom, it's not really dark yet and we were really having a lot of fun."

Charles entered the room. "Tina, where were you all this time? We have hardly seen you at all today."

"I know Dad, I'm really sorry. I just didn't realize how late it was until it was too late. I won't do it again."

Charles glanced at Lilly. "Well, you better not, or you won't see your friends for a long while."

Tina nodded and gave her parents hugs. "I think I'm going to go to bed now. I'm pretty tired. Love you both!"

She beamed a smile at them and headed off to bed.

Sherry and David sent Cody to bed so they could talk alone.

"David, what do you think is going on with that tree?" She cracked the door open a bit to make sure nobody was listening then shut it back.

"I've been thinking about it for a while now, but I'm just not getting anywhere. Maybe we should ask some people around here if they have any ideas."

Sherry scoffed at David. "Have you lost your mind David? People will think we're nuts! You can't just go around a new neighborhood that we just moved into and start telling people that the wind talks to us! And you can't tell them about the weird pictures either!" Sherry made an unpleasant face at David.

"Well I don't see *you* coming up with anything better!" They heard a knock at the door.

"Guys, its bedtime," their father said through the closed door.

"Dang, so much for talking," said Sherry. "We can get up early tomorrow and go get Tina."

David nodded and went to his room.

❧❧

Melinda woke up. "Ken?" she said in a sleepy voice.

Ken ran down the stairs. "Yeah Hon?" He stroked her hair.

"Are the kid's home?" She tried to sit up on the couch.

"Yes, they're home. They came in while you were napping. Are you ready to go to the hospital yet?"

Melinda curled her lips.

"Not really, but my foot hurts pretty bad. Is it still bleeding?" She looked at the bloody gauze wrapped around her foot.

"Not as bad as it was before, but I still think you should get stitches, just to be on the safe side." Melinda nodded.

Ken went upstairs to tell David to watch over Sherry and Cody while they were gone. "It's about an hour drive there and another hour back, so between drive time and hospital time, it might be morning before we get home. Can you handle that?"

David nodded. "Sure. Not a problem Dad. You go take care of Mom. We'll be fine." Ken patted David on the back.

"I'm sure everything will be fine. You kids should all be sleeping anyway." David agreed. Ken went back downstairs to get Melinda.

Sherry stretched out on her bed. Her room was dark and quiet. Thoughts of all that had happened went through her mind over and over. "What the heck is wrong with this place?" she thought to herself. "We've only been here a few days and already weird stuff is happening." She rolled over onto her side and tried to stop thinking about the tree and the voice but she was unsuccessful. She couldn't sleep at all. She got up and walked to her desk. "I might as well mess around on my computer until I'm ready to pass out." She turned on the computer and opened her diary.

Dear Diary. Today had to be the strangest day of my life. I met a new friend, Tina, and we got along pretty good. She's two years older than me, but I don't mind and she didn't either. We went into the woods and she showed me her secret reading place. It's really beautiful, but there's something weird about it. A lot of strange things have been happening since we went there and none of us know why.

She continued to enter all the info of the day into her diary when something even more strange happened.

"What? Why is that here?" While she was typing, her paint program popped up. "I didn't click on that!" Sherry was confused but closed the program and went back to her diary. 'There was writing on the tree that disappeared and….'

The paint program popped up again.

"I must be really tired." She closed the program again and stood up to go lay down. When she crawled into bed and glanced at the screen, there it was again.

"David!" Sherry screamed to her brother as she watched her computer do whatever it wanted.

David sprinted into the room.

"What?" He was out of breath from running down the hall.

"My computer is doing weird stuff!"

David looked at the screen. "That's just your paint program Sherry. You must have had a dream. Go back to sleep. Dad took Mom to the hospital and they won't be home until morning."

Sherry sat up in her bed. "No David, I haven't gone to sleep yet. I was just on my computer trying to write in my diary and the paint program kept coming on by itself!" David looked at her oddly.

Sherry continued. "I thought maybe I was just getting tired and imagining stuff, but when I got in bed, it did it again!"

David sat at the computer and turned the paint program off. "Sherry, you need to be cool tonight. Dad is counting on me to watch over you and Code without any problems."

David heard a beep. "What the heck?" David's eyes got huge when he looked at the screen and saw the paint program open again.

"I *told* you so! But don't listen to me, *oh, no!*" Sherry said as she wagged her finger in David's face.

David tried to click it off again, only this time the program popped back up as quickly as he closed it. "Great! My computer's possessed!" Sherry said as she rolled her eyes.

"Cut it out Sherry! There *has* to be an explanation for this." He continued to close the program as quick as it popped up but the computer seemed to be winning the game of speed.

"Yep, it's possessed and so is everything else around here!"

David got tired of Sherry's comments and stood up to confront her. "Sherry! I can't figure this out if you're going to stand behind me making stupid remarks left and right. Be quiet!"

Sherry stood there with her mouth wide open, her eyes fixed on the screen. David turned around to continue fighting with the computer. David's face turned white as a sheet. The room was quiet except for the sound of David and Sherry breathing. On the screen was a picture, it was the tree.

"Sherry, did you set your computer up to do this somehow, 'cuz if you did, it's not funny."

"No, I didn't. I have no clue how that picture showed up. You have to open a file to access the picture that Tina drew on here, and I didn't open it." David scratched his head trying to figure it out. "And besides, that's not the picture that Tina drew. Look, the lines and patterns in the background aren't there. This is a new one, David."

Sherry sat on the bed still shocked as she stared at the tree in the picture.

David tried to save the picture for proof, but the program closed the minute he tried. "Man, I wanted to print that one out and compare it to the other one!" He felt like he was unable to think straight. "Look, Sherry, whatever is going on around here may be weird and it may even be kind of scary, but try not to think about it at least until tomorrow."

Sherry agreed.

David saw the remnants of tears shining on her face as he walked towards the door. "Don't worry, it'll be okay. Just try to get some sleep. I'll stay up a little while longer so you don't feel so alone." Sherry closed her eyes as David shut the door.

❧❦

The sun rose, birds chirped and it appeared that the new day was just like any other day. Tina was sitting at the kitchen table eating her usual scrambled eggs with sausage. Lilly was ready for church, as was Charles.

"Mom, could I skip church today please?" Lilly looked at Charles assuming he would answer Tina. "I kind of told Sherry we could hang out again today." Tina grinned.

Charles chuckled. "Well, I suppose that since you go to church every other Sunday that you could miss one day."

Tina jumped up from her chair and danced around.

"Thanks Dad."

She gobbled down her eggs and ran to get dressed. Within a mere five minutes, Tina was dressed all in violet again and ran out the front door. She cut across her yard and onto the sidewalk.

"Well hi there young lady!" Mrs. King popped around from behind her apple tree.

"Hi Mrs. King! How are you today?" Tina asked in a cheerful tone.

"Oh, I'm okay I suppose. I miss my babies though."

"Your babies?" Mrs. King pointed to where her hummingbird feeder used to hang in her tree.

"Oh, the hummingbirds. Yeah, they're so cute. When will they be back again?"

Mrs. King buttoned up her sweater when a cool breeze blew by. "Not until spring I'm afraid. They don't like the cold weather."

Tina nodded. "Mrs. King? Can I ask you a question?"

"Sure honey, what's on your mind?" Tina thought of a good way to ask her question. "Well, you know the new kids that moved in down the way?"

Mrs. King glanced down the road. "I haven't had the pleasure of meeting them yet, but I have seen them out in their yard."

"Well, I took them into the woods yesterday. There's a tree there that I like to read by. Anyway, some really strange things have been going on since we went there."

Mrs. King stood up one of her garden gnomes that had fallen over. "What do you mean by strange?" She got a look of concern on her face.

"Well, we've been hearing things and…"

Mrs. King cut her off. "You know honey, I remember when I was but a little girl, my father told me I could go out for the first time alone. It was the most exciting day of my life. I remember thinking that the whole world was mine to explore. I went into those very woods that you speak of. I don't think that he expected me to wander off so far, but I did nonetheless. I remember it like it was yesterday. I walked and walked, sometimes that you simply can't explain, but that doesn't necessarily mean that it's a bad thing."

Tina nodded. "Mrs. King, you said that you stopped at the base of a tree when you gave up? What kind of a tree was it?" Tina listened closely for her reply.

"Well, it's been many years. I don't think I could tell you exactly what kind of tree, but I remember that I took shelter under the big roots."

Tina put her hand to her mouth, trying not to look frightened. "Uhm, I need to go now, I'm sorry. Thanks for telling me the story Mrs. King, but I told the new kids I would come over this morning. I really should be going."

Mrs. King smiled at Tina as she scampered across her yard to the sidewalk. "Don't be afraid child, don't be afraid," Mrs. King said quietly, as Tina ran down the sidewalk to the Parkers home.

Sherry, David and Cody finished up their breakfast. "I wonder how Mom is doing. They should have been home by now." Sherry took the breakfast dishes to the sink.

"I'm sure she's okay Sherry," David assured her, trying to keep his siblings calm.

Cody looked out the kitchen window hoping to see his parent's car pull up in the driveway. They heard a knock at the door, an urgent sounding knock.

"It's Tina," Cody said. Sherry answered the door.

"Sherry, I have *got* to talk to you."

They sat on the living room couch. "I just talked to Mrs. King. She told me a story you are *not* going to believe."

David and Cody heard the excitement in Tina's voice and joined them in the living room. "Okay, so what did she say?"

Tina looked around the house with concern "Where are your mom and dad? Didn't they come home yet?"

Sherry hung her head. "No, we don't know what happened. They should have been home by now."

Tina looked at Cody. "Oh I'm sure everything is okay. Sometimes you get stuck in emergency rooms for hours just waiting to be seen." They'll probably be home any minute now," Tina said, and David agreed.

"So what did you want to tell us about Mrs. King?"

"Oh, well, she told me a story about when she was a little girl."

Cody rolled his eyes. "Aw, I don't want to hear some old person story. Grammy tells me those all the time. Boring!"

Sherry became irritated by her little brother. "Shut up Cody! I want to hear this."

Tina continued, "She was telling me about when she was little and got lost in the woods—*these* woods."

When she was finished telling them the story, Ken and Melinda pulled up in the driveway.

"Mom and Dad are home!" yelled Cody. The kids ran out to the car to see how their Mom was.

"Are you okay, Mom?" David asked, looking at his Mom's foot as she opened the car door.

"I'm fine honey. Doc said that it was good that I went to the hospital, I really needed stitches."

Sherry hugged her mom as she stood up. "Mom, I was really worried about you."

"She's okay, guys, but she needs to stay off her foot once I get her in the house; so you guys need to keep the house tidied up okay?" said Ken.

"I washed the breakfast dishes already, Mom," said Sherry, beaming with pride.

"Thanks, Sherry, I guess I need to slow down a bit," Melinda chuckled.

Chapter 6

Mrs. King opened a drawer and pulled out an old photo album with assorted photos of family and friends taken through the years. She paged through them all, smiling as she thought back to when she was young.

As she went through the book, she pulled out a stack of tattered and folded papers. She opened one of the papers to reveal an old drawing; a drawing of a tree. Not just any tree, but the big tree that she sat at the bottom of so many years ago. She remembered drawing it the day after she got lost in the woods. Tears ran down her face as she smiled.

Melinda sat on the couch and propped her foot up.

"We're going to go upstairs, Mom. Do you need anything before we go?"

Melinda picked up one of her favorite "Better Homes and Gardens" magazines. "No honey, but thanks."

The kids ran up the stairs and into Sherry's room.

Ken walked into the living room and sat in the chair next to the couch.

"I bet you're exhausted."

"Yes, but I'm still worried about the kids."

Melinda closed the magazine.

"Honey, we talked about this in the waiting room last night. Don't do this to yourself." Ken walked over to Melinda and sat next to her on the couch to comfort her.

"Ken, why would they say they heard voices if they didn't hear them? They may be kids, but I can feel that something is wrong. They're all acting very odd."

Ken stood up. "Look Melinda, I haven't noticed any of them acting any different. You have *got* to stop freaking out about every little thing; it's not good for you." He paced back and forth.

"If you think it's just my imagination, then why don't you ask them about it yourself?"

"I never said it was your imagination Melinda, I merely said that you are getting too worked up over some silly things that the kids said. You *know* how kids make stuff up all the time. Did you get this upset when Cody went through his imaginary friend stage?" Ken shook his head as he paced the floor.

"Ken, that wasn't even the same thing. A lot of kids have imaginary friends."

"Oh come on Melinda! He wasted whole plates of food three times a day, every day for someone that wasn't really there! I didn't see you get upset about that!"

Melinda adjusted her foot to make it more comfortable. "Okay, maybe he went a bit crazy with his friend, but I'm telling you, this isn't the same. The kids were really upset about the voice they heard. They said it sounded like a voice whispering 'pillow catch'. And Tina heard it in a different place than David and Cody."

Ken sat in his chair. "Okay look—I'll go up and talk to them about it if it will make you feel better, but I really think it's nothing."

Melinda nodded and smiled.

☙ ❧

"I really think that all of this has something to do with what happened to Mrs. King. It's just too weird that she just happened to mention a big tree that had big shelter-like roots," said Tina.

Sherry nodded. "I say we go back to the tree and see if anything is different," She said as she raised her hand.

"I agree," David said.

"Agree," Cody uttered quietly.

"Agree," answered Tina.

They heard a knock at the door.

"Guys, can I come in?" asked Ken.

"Everyone quiet." Sherry whispered. She opened the door. "Yeah Dad?"

"I need to talk to you kids." Ken pushed the door open all the way and walked in. "Okay, I promised your mom that I'd talk to you about something she heard you guys talking about."

He sat on the bed. The kids stood around looking nervous.

"She says that you guys were talking about some voice you heard, like whispering? What's that all about?"

David looked at Sherry and Tina. "Well uhm, we don't really know yet Dad," David said.

Ken seemed puzzled. "What do you mean by that?"

Tina stepped forward. "Mr. Parker, uhm—Ken, some strange things have been going on since yesterday; nothing bad really, but definitely strange."

"Yeah, at first we didn't really think it was anything, but now we think it may have something to do with Mrs. King," Sherry tried to explain.

"Okay, slow down. Now what exactly has happened that you think is so strange and who is Mrs. King?" Ken listened for an answer from the kids.

Tina replied quickly. "Mrs. King is my next door neighbor. I guess I was the first one to have something weird happen to me. I was walking home from your house yesterday and I heard a whisper when the wind blew."

"Yeah, then me and David heard it when we went to the tree yesterday," said Cody.

"*And* we saw words and stuff written on the tree but when we went back with the girls, it was gone," David added.

"And Dad, I printed out a picture that Tina drew on my computer and later it was different, it looked like a photograph of something that she didn't draw," Sherry said.

"It looked like a picture of the tree, the same tree that I drew at my house yesterday that came out looking like a photograph," Tina said.

"Okay, wait a minute. You guys are all talking about some tree, what tree? Where?" asked Ken.

"My secret reading spot," said Tina "They're talking about the place I've been going to since I was little. It's in the woods. I took Sherry there yesterday to show it to her and weird stuff has been happening ever since."

Ken rubbed his chin. "Uh huh. And where exactly is this tree?"

"I couldn't tell you really, but I could show you," replied Tina.

Ken approved.

"Sherry, why don't you show him the pictures," Tina suggested.

Sherry walked over to her desk and took the pictures to her father.

"Here Dad, look for yourself."

Ken held the two pictures up and inspected them. "Which one was printed here?" David pointed.

"That one Dad, and you can tell 'cuz in the background is the actual drawing that Tina made."

Ken gazed at the pictures.

"This *is* odd," he said as he tried to make sense of the identical pictures. "And you said you drew this other one at home, Tina?".

"Yes sir. I drew it with my colored pencils, but it came out looking like someone took a picture of the tree with a camera."

"And the voice, what did you say that it said?"

"Pillow catch," chimes Cody.

"Cody, we're not sure if that's what it is or not, but it's something like that."

Ken put the pictures down on the bed. "Pillow catch?" Ken looked at the kids with one eyebrow raised.

"Dad, to tell you the truth, we have no clue. All we know is that we hear it when the wind blows and it's like a whisper, but it's definitely a voice," said David.

"David, you have to understand how odd this whole thing sounds. I mean, it sounds like a fantasy to me. Just like the stories I try to write." Ken stood up.

"I know Dad, but you saw the pictures yourself and you can't deny that it's downright strange," David replied.

"Well, then I guess we need to go to the tree and see if we can figure this whole thing out."

The kids took Ken to the woods; hoping that something would happen while he was there to prove that he wasn't just the victim of four very overactive imaginations.

As they walked through the woods toward Tina's secret reading spot, Ken looked up at the size of the trees in awe. He couldn't help but wonder how old they were.

"Man, these are some old trees," he said as he rubbed his hand down the trunk of one of them.

"These are nothing, just wait 'til you see the reading spot," said Sherry jokingly.

Ken observed as they walked that the grass and foliage seemed to get greener and more beautiful. They finally saw the tree up ahead. Ken stared ahead as if his eyes were fixed to the tree.

"This is it Dad. Pretty cool huh?" said Cody.

"This is unbelievable! This thing has to be thousands of years old and it looks a lot bigger here than it did in the pictures you showed me," Ken declared as he looked at the huge roots jutting out from the side of the tree.

Tina crawled under the tree roots. "This is where I read my Harry Potter books."

Ken walked over to the shelter. "I can see why you like it here Tina, it's very pretty."

The wind changed directions and gusted a bit faster.

"Show me where you saw writing on the tree David," Ken said as he searched the massive tree trunk.

"Over here Dad," David said. He and Cody pointed to the exact spot that the words were written.

"Do you remember what it said?" asked Ken.

"Yeah, it said 'We swear our silence.'"

Ken was overwhelmed by all the odd things going on.

"And over here were initials, I think they were C.D. and L.L., but I'm not sure."

Ken checked both spots on the tree where David and Cody saw the writing, but found nothing. "I don't know what to tell you kids, but there's nothing here. Maybe you just thought you saw something."

"Dad, Tina and I didn't see it, but we really believe that David and Cody DID see it. You have to believe us," cried Sherry as she looked at her father with tearful eyes.

At that moment, the wind changed directions again. The branches and leaves in the trees all around them danced as if they were happy to see them. The voice within the wind spoke and they all heard it.

"wiiillllooowwwww....paaaattccchhhh."

They all stared at each other, ready to run if needed.

"Whoa! Did you guys hear that?" asked David, looking as if he just rode on a wild roller coaster.

Ken replied. "Yes, I certainly did. And it didn't say 'pillow catch' either. It said 'willow patch.'"

Ken laughed at the very idea that he actually heard a mysterious voice in the wind.

"So, now what should we do Dad?" asked Cody.

"Well Code man, I really don't know, but I do know this, I have to get back home and check on your mother."

"But Dad! We can't just leave now!" Sherry said as she held her father's arm.

"Sherry, I know this is important to you right now, and I have to say that I am even intrigued, but I have to make sure your mom is okay. I can't just leave her there alone for too long with a messed up foot. What if she needs something?" Ken started walking out of the woods. "I'll come back in a little bit; just let me check on her real quick."

Sherry nodded realizing that her father was right.

"Guys, what do you suppose willow patch means?" asked Tina as she looked at the leaves blowing in the tree.

"I don't know, maybe a place?" said David, uncertain of his answer.

"Could be. Maybe we should look around this whole area more; ya know maybe something else around here will be the key to this whole thing," Tina said as she walked deeper into the woods, looking for answers.

"Tina! Wait up!" yelled Sherry. "The only things that are really disturbing about this whole situation are the pictures and the writing on the tree that disappeared."

David and Cody lagged behind the girls as they searched the woods.

Chapter 7

Charles and Lilly came home from church.

"Want me to fix you some lunch?" Lilly asked her husband.

"Sure, something light would be nice, maybe a salad?"

Lilly opened the refrigerator and pulled out a bag of precut lettuce and poured it in a bowl.

"So where do you suppose our little princess is today?" Charles questioned as he turned the pages of the Sunday paper.

"Remember dear? She said this morning she was going out to play with the new kids down the street."

Lilly brought a bowl of salad to her husband.

"Ah yes, off on more adventures I guess," he said with a smile.

"Yes, I suppose. I hope she doesn't come in too late again," Lilly replied looking rather uneasy.

"What's wrong?" Charles asked, seeing that Lilly was distraught.

"What if she goes *there* Charles?"

Charles stood up and walked to the kitchen. "I need crackers to go with my salad." Lilly followed him.

"Charles? What if she goes there?"

Charles sighed. "Then we must forbid her to ever go into the woods again."

"Oh Charles, you know how much Tina loves the woods and the animals. She would just die if we did that to her. It's bad enough that we never got her a dog when she wanted one. At least she can see animals in the woods."

Charles walked back to the living room with crackers in hand. "Lilly, we both know that the chances of her finding that place are pretty slim, considering the size of the woods. If she did by chance go there and we knew, we would have no choice but to forbid her to ever go again. It could be dangerous."

Lilly nodded as she sat in her chair. "But how would we ever know if she *had* been there?" Lilly questioned.

"We'd know; she'd tell us, believe me." Charles opened his paper back and began to read.

❧❧

Ken and Melinda sat on the couch talking. Ken told Melinda what he heard in the woods.

"I'm telling you, I could not believe it. There I was standing with the kids when all of a sudden I hear this voice saying 'willow patch'. It was the weirdest thing I have ever experienced."

Melinda sipped her tea as Ken told the whole story.

"I thought they were all just imagining this. I mean, you told me what they said in the bedroom, but I never thought any of it was true." Ken shook his head in disbelief.

"So where are the kids now Ken?" Melinda asked.

"They stayed at the tree while I came here to check on you."

Melinda was shocked. "You mean you left them there alone after you heard the voice?"

"Well yes, but—I don't think there is anything to worry about, Melinda. I get a peaceful feeling there. I can't really explain it. It's almost spiritual," Ken said with a smile.

"Well, I think you need to get back out there just in case. You don't know what might happen," Melinda said as she pointed at the front door.

Ken agreed and headed back to the woods. "I hope I can find it again", he thought to himself as he walked out the door.

⋞⋟

"I'm getting hungry, David," Cody whined as the four walked through the deep woods looking for clues.

"Cody, we'll go back in a little bit, but right now this is really important," David said as he moved low-hanging branches out of the way.

Sherry crawled over a huge stump in the ground from a tree that had fallen years ago. "Ouch!" Sherry screamed in pain.

"Sherry! Are you okay?" Tina yelled as she watched her friend tumble to the ground.

"Darn tree stump!" Sherry looked down to see a big knot in her leg where she scraped the tree as she fell.

"That doesn't look good, Sherry," David said when he caught up and looked at her leg. "Can you stand on it?"

Sherry pulled up on David, but she wasn't able to put pressure on it.

"Ouch!" she yelled again. Cody started to sob. "Great, now what do we do?" asked Sherry in an angry tone.

"I guess I'll have to carry you. Sure hope you didn't eat too much breakfast," David joked to lighten the situation.

"Oh very funny, David!" said Sherry.

Tina looked at the sky. "We better hurry guys; your Dad was supposed to be coming back, remember?"

"Geez, not only do I have to carry you, but I have to run!" David laughed.

They tried to find their way back to the giant tree and Ken. Sherry groaned in pain as David lugged her over top of big tree stumps and various plants.

"David, thanks for doing this. I mean—you didn't have to," Sherry said, seeing how difficult it was for David.

"No biggie Sherry. Besides, you'd make a terrible tasting snack for a bear."

Sherry laughed hard as David continued walking through the thick woods looking for the tree.

❦

"Hello? Guys! Where are you?" Ken yelled for the kids to no avail. He looked all around the huge tree hoping to catch a glimpse of one of them, but found nothing. "Sherry! David! Cody! Tina!" He searched frantically for them, hearing his wife's voice in his head the whole time. 'You mean you left them there alone?' It was rough hearing those words but he knew she was right. He felt horrible and wanted so badly to find the kids.

Chapter 8

Melinda searched through the phonebook for the Brooks' phone number. Her finger glided across the page. "Brahm, Breck, Brigam, Brooks. Allen Brooks. Betty Brooks. Charles Brooks. Here we go."

She dialed the phone on the table next to the couch. "Hello. Is this Lilly Brooks?"

"Yes," the voice on the other end replied.

"This is Melinda Parker, we just moved in down the way."

"Oh yes, Melinda. How are you?" responded Lilly.

"Well, I was just wondering if you by any chance know of any strange happenings around here."

The line was quiet for a few seconds.

"Uhm—I'm not sure if I understand what you are asking," Lilly said, with hesitation in her voice.

"Lilly, our kids, including Tina, have been talking about voices that they are hearing. They took my husband out to the woods to show him a tree where some odd things have been happening. Now, I don't know if your daughter told you and your husband anything, but I figured you should know about it if she didn't." Silence filled the line once again. "Lilly?" Melinda tried to get her to reply.

"Yes—yes I heard you Melinda," Lilly said, sounding very frightened.

"Anyway, I just thought I should call you and let you know and see if you knew about anything ever happening around here."

"Melinda, some things are best kept as secrets," Lilly said.

"What are you talking about? Do you know something Lilly? Please tell me because right now, my family and your daughter are all out there somewhere in the woods trying to figure this whole thing out," Melinda said in a rather frantic tone.

"I'm sorry Melinda, but my husband and I 'swore our silence'."

Lilly hung up the phone. Melinda looked at the receiver of the phone and slammed it down.

~ઉ৯~

"David! Cody! Sherry! Tina!" Ken yelled at the top of his lungs. "I should've taken them back home with me. I shouldn't have left them here!" He looked to the sky. "Please let them be okay."

Clouds began to gather above him, looking like a storm was approaching. He could feel the dampness in the air as he trudged along, deeper and deeper into the woods.

~ઉ৯~

David looked tired and Sherry was starting to lose hope that they would ever find their way back.

"David, sit down and take a break, you've been carrying me for like an hour." Sherry said sympathetically.

"I can't stop Sherry, I can't waste any time. I just wish I had a compass or something with me. I think I already passed that tree with the red flowers once. Or maybe it was just another one that looks like it. I'm so confused."

David was exhausted but tried hard to take care of the other three kids.

Tina looked at the sky. "I think we're going west."

David looked up. "How can you tell?"

"Because the sun rises in the east and sets in the west. When it's noon it's straight up above us, but it's past there because it's setting now. We're heading in the direction that the sun is, which is west." Tina smiled at David.

"Well, that's what I get for asking stupid questions." David chuckled. "Cody, how ya doin' back there buddy?" David asked his brother.

"I'm hungry! Can we please go home?"

Tina walked over to a bush and started rummaging through it. "Here Cody." She handed him a handful of fresh raspberries. "These are really good. I used to eat these when I came out to read." Cody gobbled down the raspberries.

"Thanks Tina," Cody said as he wiped the juice from his hands onto his pants.

"Okay, now that we have Cody's stomach under control, lets see if we can find Dad or the tree," David said as he yanked Sherry up higher onto his back.

Tina kept watch over the sky and the direction they were going.

"David, do you think Dad is looking for us?" Sherry asked, sounding worried and tired.

"I'm sure he is Sherry. If Dad says he'll be back, he means it."

∽᳝᳝

Lilly practiced her music for the upcoming concert at Middleton Centre. She hit a sour note and tossed her bow to the floor.

"Come on! You can play better than this!" she reprimanded herself.

Charles walked into the bedroom. "Don't be so hard on yourself."

Lilly picked up the music and showed it to her husband.

"Look at this! I can't do it! I have tried and tried and it seems like the longer I practice, the worse I sound!"

Charles took the sheet music and put it back on her stand.

"Honey, you never get this temperamental when you practice. What's wrong?"

"It's this whole tree thing Charles. I got a call from Melinda Parker a while ago," she said.

"Melinda Parker?" asked Charles.

"The new family down the street? Remember?"

"Oh yes. Sorry. What did she want?"

Lilly stood up and paced the floor. "She asked me if I knew about any strange goings on around here. She said that all of her kids and Tina have been talking about voices and a big tree. She said that they are all out there right now with Ken, her husband."

Charles nodded his head.

"Charles, our daughter is out there! We have to do something!" Lilly started to cry.

"I'll go, you stay here."

He started to walk out of the room when Lilly stopped him.

"I'm going with you!"

"No, it might be dangerous Lilly. Our daughter is already out there, I can't take a chance on something happening to both of you."

Charles left the room as Lilly sobbed quietly.

The air became cooler and it started to rain. Ken parted the vines hanging from a tree as he saw the massive tree in the distance.

"Kids! Sherry! David! Cody! Tina! Someone please answer me! Where are you?"

Ken walked toward the tree hoping to find at least one of the kids safe near the huge roots, but that wasn't the case. He sat by the tree thinking that they would come back. As he sat there, tears rolled down his face, mixing in with the raindrops. He heard the voice.

"Wiiilllloooowwww paaaattccchhhhhh."

After hours of looking for the kids, knowing that he had left his injured wife at home to find them, Ken snapped. "What do you want? What is willow patch and why do you keep saying it? Where are my children? Tell me!" Ken cried, getting no answer in reply to his series of questions.

❧

· Charles walked through the wet woods. He tried to remember the exact location of the secret place he and Lilly once visited years ago. He pressed on to find the tree where his princess and new neighbors were. The rain became heavy; lightning lit up the sky. Low rumbling could be heard in the distance.

He finally arrived at the tree where he found Ken sitting on the ground, drenched and crying.

"I suppose you're Ken? I'm Charles. Charles Brooks. Where are the children?"

Ken stood up and shook hands with Charles.

"Thank God, some help. I can't find them. They were here before I went back to check on my wife, but when I returned, they were gone. I told them I would come right back. I don't know where they went." Ken hung his head.

"None of you should have ever come here!" Charles snapped at Ken.

"Hey! It was your daughter that showed this place to our kids! They wouldn't have ever come here if it wasn't for Tina." Ken slowly lowered his tone as he yelled back at Charles, knowing that he couldn't possibly blame Tina for this. Charles backed off as well.

"Tina? My Tina brought them here?" A look of embarrassment rushed over Charles' face. "I—I'm so sorry. I didn't know," he said apologetically.

Ken patted Charles on the arm. "It's okay; I guess we're a lot alike. Protective dads." Ken laughed. Charles smiled at Ken.

"Okay, let's go find our kids." said Charles.

They walked off to look for them as the rain poured down.

"David! Cody! Tina! Sherry!" Charles and Ken yelled as loud as they could, trying to be heard over the loud thunder and rain.

❧❧

The kids sat on a large rock resting their tired feet. The sky lit up all around them.

"I'm cold, David," complained Cody, shivering and soaking wet.

"I know, Cody. I'm sorry; I needed to take a break."

Tina and Sherry huddled together for warmth. "Tina?" said Sherry.

"Yes?"

"I'm sorry we messed up your reading spot." Sherry said shaking all over.

"What do you mean Sherry? You didn't mess it up." Sherry looked at Tina sadly.

"You said that nothing strange ever happened until we came here. How do you explain that?" Tina wiped the tears from Sherry's face and replied.

"Sherry, I don't know what is going on, but I can tell you this, it's not your fault. I would never blame any of you for this. I'm so lucky that your family moved in. I never had any friends until you guys came." Sherry smiled at Tina.

"You really mean it?"

"Yes, I was so lonely; then you moved in and now I have a best friend."

Sherry hugged Tina.

"Thanks Tina. You're a great friend. I haven't known you long, but already, you're a better friend than any I have ever known."

They watched the lightning light up the woods, hoping it would help them to find their way to the tree.

"Time to get moving again," said David.

Charles and Ken continued looking for the kids as the sky become darker, and the night got colder.

"Charles, have you heard the voice before?" Ken asked with a shaky voice.

Charles glanced at Ken briefly. "Yes, I have."

"When did you hear it?" Ken asked.

"It was long ago, before we had Tina. See, we used to live here when we first got married. The house we're in now belonged to my uncle. He gave it to us as a wedding present and he moved to the city."

Ken nodded as he listened.

"So why did you move away?"

"We were young and stupid. We eloped one night before we had even gone to college. Once we realized that we still had to go to college if we were ever to make a life for ourselves and our children, we decided to move close to the college of our choice. Once we had graduated from college and Lilly had become pregnant, we were broke and had no choice but to move back here."

Ken tried to soak up the whole story. "So when did you hear the voice?" he asked again.

"Before we went off to college. We went for a long walk in the woods. We wanted to enjoy the beauty of it all before we left. I remember walking with Lilly, it was wonderful. She was my new wife and I loved her so much. We found a nice shady spot to relax and talk. Lilly decided to carve our initials in the tree as a sign of our love for one another. Then it happened."

Ken stopped walking to hear the end of the story.

Charles continued. "A voice came out of nowhere and said 'willow patch'. It scared the life out of Lilly; and I— well I had to maintain composure, but I was quite frightened myself."

Ken was amazed. "So it does say 'willow patch.'"

"Yes, we are quite sure that was what it said. But it wasn't finished. When we started to run away, we heard it again. 'Swear your silence.' We thought that if we said that we swore our silence about what we heard, that it would be content, but we were wrong. It kept repeating that same sentence over and over until we saw a light shining on the tree. It was there that Lilly and I decided to carve into the tree that we swore our silence. That was the last time that we heard anything. We left for college the next day and didn't return until twelve years ago."

Ken resumed walking and looking for the kids, the rain still pouring down.

"We told Tina to always be in by dark, but never thought she would find this place."

Ken mulled over Charles' story as they searched for their children.

"So the initials, the ones that the kids saw on the tree. Those were made by you and Lilly?" Ken asked.

"Yes. Lilly carved L.L. since her maiden name was Lundgren," answered Charles.

"But the boys were the only ones that saw them. When they tried to show the girls and me where they were on the tree, we couldn't find them. How do you explain that?"

Ken waited for an answer. Charles looked up into the dark sky as he walked.

"I don't know my friend. I just don't know."

Chapter 9

Melinda heard a knock on her front door.

"Hello? I—I'm sorry, I can't come to the door. You'll have to let yourself in," Melinda answered nervously, thinking she could be calling a burglar or worse into her home.

Lilly peeked in through the door. "Melinda? It's Lilly. Can I come in for a few minutes?"

Melinda, although in pain, and worried, found the company of Lilly comforting as Melinda waited for Ken and the kids.

"Sure Lilly, have a seat." Melinda motioned for Lilly to sit down in Ken's chair.

Lilly had a distraught look on her face.

"Melinda, have you heard anything more from Ken or anyone?" Lilly asked in hopes of good news.

"I'm afraid I haven't, but I'm sure Ken will find them." Melinda tried to sound positive.

Lilly noticed that Melinda was injured and that her tea cup was empty.

"Can I get you a fresh cup of tea? I know it must be hard for you alone here with in your condition. "

Melinda smiled.

"That would be very nice Lilly. You'll find the tea bags in a container on the counter. The teapot is on the stove."

Lilly walked into the kitchen, noticing how perfectly clean everything was.

"Your home is beautiful Melinda. You must spend a lot of time keeping it up like this with three children."

Melinda grinned. "Yes well, it is difficult. Our three are a handful, but cleaning is like second nature to me."

Lilly filled the teapot with water and put it on the stove to heat up. "So what happened to your foot?" Lilly was curious.

"Oh, it was silly. I was doing dishes and dropped a plate on my foot. Ken took me in for stitches, but the doctor told me to stay off of it for a while," Melinda replied.

"Melinda?" Lilly called from the kitchen.

"Yes Lilly?"

"I'm sorry for being so short with you on the phone earlier," Lilly said, sounding embarrassed.

"Oh that's okay. I understand." Melinda reassured Lilly that she wasn't upset about it.

Lilly walked out and set the fresh cup of tea on the table. "Here you go," said Lilly with a smile. Melinda glanced up at Lilly as she picked up the cup.

"I really hope the kids are okay. I mean, I'm not from around here, so I really don't know how safe it is." Melinda tried not to sound as if the area were untrustworthy.

"Well, with both of our husbands out there, I'm sure they'll be found. We just have to be patient," Lilly said, trying to stay calm.

The Beginning

≪⌘⌘≫

David breathed hard as he carried his sister along the dark path within the woods.

"I can't believe how dark it is out here. This is like, darker than my bedroom at night."

Tina heard a sound. "Did you guys hear that?"

David stopped and listened. Cody stopped in his tracks.

"What? What did you hear Tina?" asked Sherry.

"Wow! That was really strange. It was like a tinkling bell sound," Tina replied.

David set Sherry down on the ground and took another break. "I don't hear anything Tina. Maybe it was just a bug or something flying by your ear."

Sherry rubbed her ankle as she tried to hear the noise. They all sat quietly together listening intently.

"Wait! I heard something!" said Cody looking surprised. A wisp of light flew by the children. "Did you see that?" David jumped up onto his tired feet. Tina stood up.

"Yes I did! And I heard the sound again too! What was that?" Tina asked as she watched the woods around them.

Sherry tried to stand up. "It buzzed right passed me guys! If that's a bug I sure hope it doesn't bite!"

David tried to get the situation under control. "Okay guys, we're getting a little jumpy here. It was probably some strange type of lightning bug or something. You know how the queen bee is so much bigger than the rest of the bees? That was probably like the queen lightning bug."

Sherry looked at David in disbelief. "So you think that was the queen lightning bug?" Sherry rolled her eyes.

"Well, I don't really know what it was, but it's gone, so let's get moving before it comes back," David commanded. He pulled Sherry back onto his back and started leading the group through the darkness.

"David, do you think Mom is okay?" Cody asked his big brother.

"I'm sure she's fine Code. She's safe at home. Besides I bet the only thing on her mind right now is where we are."

Cody picked at his finger as he walked, looking worried.

"There it is again!" yelled Sherry as she ducked her head down onto David's shoulder.

"Whoa! That was *no* bug!" yelled Cody. The sound was louder that time, and the light brighter.

"What the heck *is* that David?!" asked Sherry.

Tina watched closely as the creature seemed to quickly fly by David and Sherry over and over again. David tried to duck down as it flew closer to him and Sherry. Cody hid behind a tree. The kids frantically tried to dodge the foreign flying object as it darted to and fro.

"No, wait!" Tina yelled to David and Sherry.

David looked at Tina. "Wait for what?" he yelled back to her.

"I don't think it wants to hurt us."

David, still ducking down, replied to Tina. "Doesn't want to hurt us? We don't even know what it is!"

Tina watched and listened closely. Cody shivered behind the tree, hoping Tina was right. David tried to straighten his back as a pain grabbed him from carrying his sister for too long. Sherry heard the tinkling bell sound rush toward her.

"Look," Tina whispered to them. Sherry stiffened up as she saw the light land on her shoulder. David tried to remain calm.

"David, I'm scared," Sherry whispered in David's ear.

"Just try to stay still Sherry. If you move too quickly, you might frighten it."

Cody watched from behind the tree as the light sat upon his sister's shoulder.

Chapter 10

Charles and Ken stepped over a dead tree while they yelled as loudly as possible for the children. "Tina! Cody! Sherry! David!" They both bellowed in hopes of hearing a reply from at least one of them.

"Charles, exactly how far out do these woods go?" Ken asked.

Charles scratched his head. "Well, if I remember right it's about fifty square miles or so."

Ken kicked a stone out of the way. "Fifty miles? They could be anywhere out here!" Ken said in a huff.

"Look Ken, I know it seems like an impossible journey, but we can't just give up. These are our kids and we have to be strong for them," Charles said in a stern voice.

"I wasn't suggesting we stop looking. I would never even think about that! I'm just worried," Ken said, feeling a bit silly having even asked. "The only thing I worry about is the cold. None of them were dressed warm enough to withstand an entire night out here."

Ken tried to remember what each of his kids were wearing when he last saw them. He started imagining them huddled together, freezing in the darkness.

"Why didn't I demand they come back home with me earlier today? They'd be safe at home right now if I had," Ken scolded himself.

"It doesn't help us at all right now to beat ourselves up over mistakes. We have to just keep positive and continue looking," Charles replied.

Melinda sipped her warm tea and thought about her children. "Lilly, did something horrible happen to you in the woods? I mean, our phone call—you sounded so upset. It was like you were trying to cover something up. I really need to know the truth."

Lilly glanced at the beautiful pictures of Melinda and Ken's family on the walls.

"I know, and I am truly sorry for sounding so short with you on the phone. That's really why I stopped by."

"No, it's okay Lilly. I just need to understand what happened to you. The kids are all out there and now, our husbands too. I'm just so worried," Melinda replied.

"I know. I can't say that I'm not worried as well," Lilly said with a bit of fear in her voice.

"So what did you mean when you said that you swore your silence when we were on the phone earlier? To whom? And why?" Melinda asked.

Lilly picked at her cuticles as she answered Melinda's difficult question. "Well, it was a very long time ago Melinda. Charles and I were very young."

Melinda adjusted herself on the couch and listened.

"I—I don't know if I should even tell you this. We swore we would never speak of it."

"Lilly, I don't understand what you are talking about, but if there is someone dangerous out there, you need to tell me now. I don't care what you swore. These are our families we're talking about." Melinda started to get impatient.

"I know Melinda, but you weren't there and you can't understand how we felt or how it feels now that it's happening again," Lilly said nervously.

Lilly stood up and started pacing back and forth as she began to tell Melinda the whole truth about what happened.

⋘⋙

David and Sherry were frozen in their tracks as the light on Sherry's shoulder became brighter.

"Look at how beautiful it is," Tina whispered to Sherry, who was too afraid to even move, let alone speak. Cody's eyes lit up as he watched the light grow stronger.

"David, what is that? I feel something strange," Sherry whispered very quietly in David's ear.

"I don't know but I feel it too. A kind of tingling sensation," David replied to Sherry quietly.

Tina could not believe what she was witnessing as she stood there in the darkness. The light began to dim as the creature flew off into the night and the words 'willow patch' were heard. David straightened up as Sherry slid off his back.

"David! My ankle! It doesn't hurt anymore!" Sherry shrieked as her feet touched the ground.

Tina was astonished as she watched her friend walk like she was never hurt.

"My back doesn't hurt anymore either!" said David.

Cody crept out from behind the tree. "Is it gone? Is it okay to come out now?"

"Yes Cody, you can come out now," said Tina with a smile.

"Okay, so what was that and what just happened?" David asked with great curiosity.

Sherry looked at her ankle for any sign of swelling. "I don't know, but whatever it was healed my ankle. It's not swollen or anything now. It's just like new!" Sherry walked over to Tina. "There was *nothing* like that in our old neighborhood!"

Tina laughed. "Well I'm just as stunned as you are. As long as I have been coming out here, I have never seen anything like that!"

The girls hugged each other and giggled.

David twisted and turned, amazed at how good his back felt. "That had to be the strangest thing that has ever happened to me, seriously."

Sherry laughed. "No kidding David?"

David grinned at his sister. "Okay smarty pants, we need to get moving and try to find our way home."

They gathered back together and began walking, hoping that they'd eventually find their way out of the woods.

"I'm hungry again," Cody piped up.

"Yeesh," said David, Sherry and Tina together.

☙❧

Charles and Ken grew weary as they climbed over assorted wild plants and dead trees in search of the children.

"So, what do you think the voice was all about back then Charles?" Ken struck up a conversation to make the trudging seem easier.

"I really don't know. It's not something you hear every day. I mean, who would expect to hear a voice come from a tree? Or possibly out of thin air? I wish I knew."

Ken tried to imagine what Charles and Lilly must have felt back then. "When I heard it earlier today, it sounded mystical. Like no voice I have ever heard before. But strangely enough it didn't really frighten me. It was almost soothing. I guess that's one of the reasons I wasn't concerned about leaving the children out here alone." Charles nodded. "It wasn't dark yet and it was still warm and...."

Charles stopped Ken. "Ken, nobody is laying blame on you. Sometimes things just happen for whatever reason. I know you didn't mean any harm. Besides, you were worried about your wife as well, so you had a lot on your mind. I understand that." Charles patted Ken on the back.

"Thanks Charles. That means a lot to me. This whole thing has been so strange. I'm glad I've got you to help me out here."

Charles smiled at Ken.

The Beginning

Melinda tried to get up from the couch to make a quick run to the bathroom. "Ouch!" She mumbled under her breath. Lilly ran to help her.

"Melinda you can't walk around with your foot like that." Lilly tried to get Melinda to sit back down.

"I need to use the bathroom, but my foot is killing me," Melinda replied.

"Look, we have a wheelchair at our house that has been there ever since Charles' uncle passed away. I'm going to run and get it for you. I'll be right back."

Lilly made sure Melinda wasn't going to try to walk alone, and then ran out the front door. As she quickly made her way back to her home, she looked out toward the woods. Her thoughts turned dark as she remembered the day she and Charles heard the voice. She said a prayer as she walked down the dark road.

⤠⤟

David, still leading the group through the darkness, was feeling better, but completely lost. "I can't tell which way we're going or anything anymore," he said, sounding aggravated and tired.

"You're doing fine David," Tina assured him.

"Yeah, David, I have to say that I never thought that you could ever be a leader like this. I'm really proud of you."

David got a big smile on his face.

"But don't go and get a swollen head, you're still a dork," Sherry added.

They all had a good laugh as they walked forward into the darkness.

"Have you guys noticed that it seems to be getting warmer out here?" Tina asked.

"I have," said Cody.

"Yeah, me too," said Sherry.

"It feels like the temperature's gone up 20 degrees. That's unusual for this time of year," Tina observed.

David took notice of the change. "You don't suppose it's getting close to morning do you? I mean, it would start warming up as morning got closer wouldn't it?"

"Not really David. It doesn't usually warm up around here until the sun is actually up. Besides, it can't possibly be close to morning. Even though we've been out here a long time, it hasn't been *that* long," Tina tried to explain.

"Then why is it getting so warm in the middle of the night out here in the woods?" David asked.

Tina had no viable answer. "I wish I knew David. I'm just accepting it as a blessing considering the situation we're in."

They continued walking, when all of a sudden they all came to a complete halt.

❧❦

Lilly returned to Melinda with the wheelchair. "Here you go. Let me help you in so you can get to the bathroom," Lilly said as she helped pull Melinda into the wheelchair.

"Thank you so much for your help Lilly. I appreciate it so much," Melinda said with a smile.

"Not a problem," replied Lilly. Melinda headed for the bathroom. Lilly wandered around the living room looking at all the beautiful decorations within the home. "Are you okay in there Melinda?" Lilly yelled to her.

"I'm fine. Thanks," Melinda replied. Lilly noticed a CD carousel and began to flip through the assorted music. One CD was her favorite. The bathroom door opened and Melinda rolled back toward the couch. "Well, that took forever." Melinda quipped as she struggled to maneuver the bulky wheelchair. Lilly helped Melinda back onto the couch.

"I see you have a nice assortment of music. You even have one of my favorites," Lilly smiled at Melinda.

"Oh really, which one?" asked Melinda. Lilly brought the CD to Melinda to show her.

"Oh, that one," Melinda said.

"I love that CD. I listen to it all the time at home. I think it is absolutely beautiful music." Lilly thought of the music in her mind.

"Really? I'm not that thrilled with it," Melinda said.

Lilly looked shocked considering Melinda owned the CD.

"But why?" Lilly asked Melinda.

"Because I wrote it," Melinda replied.

Lilly looked at the cover of the CD and saw the credits containing Melinda Thompson. "Melinda Thompson. Is that you?" Lilly asked.

"Yes. That's my maiden name. I used to compose a lot of music back then."

Lilly looked confused. "But why did you stop? Your music is wonderful."

"I stopped when Ken and I got married. I thought that trying to raise a family along with composing music would have been too much for me. Besides, Ken needs me to be here on the home front for him and the kids."

Lilly shook her head. "Melinda, you have a gift. You can't just let it go like that. Don't you miss it at all?"

Melinda nodded her head. "Actually I do miss it and I would like to compose again, but right now I can't even think about that."

Although Lilly was amazed that she found her new neighbor to be one of her favorite composers, she dropped the subject.

༄ൟ

Ken and Charles sifted through the woods with a fine- tooth comb.

"I wonder how far they could have gotten in this much time. It's been hours since I have seen them," Ken said.

"Yes, but remember, they have shorter legs," Charles said with a grin.

Ken chuckled. "I suppose you're right. And Cody has some really short legs, so they can't be moving that fast," Ken replied trying to keep his spirits up.

Charles spotted something up ahead of them. "Did you see that Ken?"

"See what? What did I miss?"

"There was a light for a moment, up there ahead of us." Charles tried to focus on the area up ahead.

"Where is it now? Was it maybe a flashlight?" Ken asked.

"No, I don't think it was a flashlight. It was too high up to be a flashlight. And it moved faster than someone carrying a flashlight."

Charles and Ken kept their eyes peeled for any more light in the darkness.

"Maybe someone is out here messing with fireworks or something," Ken said.

"No, nobody would come all the way out here and shoot off fireworks. Not the right time of year and there aren't any kids out here except our four kids," Charles answered.

"That's true," said Ken.

"The light was more of a glow, not any kind of intense bright light like a firework or a flashlight," Charles explained.

Ken nodded. "Come on, we need to keep moving. I'm even getting cold out here. I can't imagine how those kids must be feeling right now."

༒

"Tina, can I have some more berries?" Cody asked.

"If I see any along the way I'll give you some Cody, but it'll be hard to find them in the dark. I'm sorry you're so hungry. Hopefully we'll get out of these woods soon," Tina tried to comfort Cody.

"Do you think Dad is still out here, David?" Sherry asked.

"I'm sure he is Sherry. He doesn't give up on anything easily, especially us. You know that."

Sherry agreed. "Yeah, he's a great dad. I miss him and Mom so much." Sherry thought about all the fun her family had in the past. A small tear formed in the corner of her eye.

"I think we'll be okay guys, really," said Tina in a positive tone.

"You really think so?" Cody asked.

"Yep, something tells me that we're going to be home before too long."

David stopped. "Hey! There it is again!"

Tina glanced around in the dark. "What? That glowie thing?"

Cody perked up.

"Yeah, I just saw it a second ago. It was about twenty feet ahead of us." David pointed ahead of them.

"I think we should head that way then David," said Sherry.

David looked at Sherry with concern. "Are you serious? Do you want a second close encounter tonight? Because I don't. The first time was freaky enough for me." David looked back in the direction of the light.

"It may have been weird or freaky, but it helped us. You know it and so do I David. If it wanted to hurt us, it could have."

Tina agreed with Sherry.

"Yeah David. Whatever it is, it seems to be trying to help us, not hurt us."

David pondered the thought of following the light. "Okay. But if it comes back and like, sucks out our brains or something, it's *not* my fault!"

Tina and Sherry busted out laughing. David started walking in the direction of the light. Tina found a few berries as they brushed against her ankle along the way and gave them to Cody.

"Yum!" Cody shouted with excitement of having something to munch on.

"I hope that will hold your stomach off for a while," Tina said with a smile.

"Okay, I just saw it again. Its right up there," David said.

"Keep following it David," Tina hollered, sure that it was trying to help them.

They walked faster, trying to keep up with the tiny glow in the distance. They could hear the slight tinkling sound it emitted as it flew.

"Faster David!" Sherry squealed, thinking they were going to lose sight of it.

"I can't go any faster Sherry or I'll lose Cody," David replied. He tried to keep sight of the glowing creature, but walked slow enough for Cody.

❧❦

Ken spotted the same light that Charles spoke of earlier.

"I see it! It's about sixty feet ahead of us. Or at least I think it is. It's hard to tell in all this darkness," Ken said, trying to judge how far it was.

"Try to keep your eye on it. I think maybe we should keep heading in that direction," Charles said.

They sped up their pace as they saw intermittent glimpses of the light through the trees.

"So Ken, is your wife going to be okay? Did the doctor say how long she has to stay off her feet?" Charles asked, remembering Melinda was home alone.

"Well, the damage wasn't really bad, but it was bad enough that she needed stitches. Doc said she just needs to stay off of it for a few days."

"Well I'm glad to hear that. I look forward to meeting her someday," Charles replied.

"Yeah, we should all get together sometime for a barbecue or something," Ken said, in hopes of their families being close.

"That would be really nice Ken. I'm sure our wives will get along just fine."

Ken wondered why Charles didn't mention how well he and Charles got along. "That's true, and you and I seem to be doing fine. I mean if we weren't panicking over where our kids are," Ken said, hoping to show Charles that he would like to be good friends as well.

Charles laughed.

"Yes, well then again, if it weren't for our kids being lost, we might not have ever met. I don't think I have ever seen any of the other residents on our street besides Mrs. King."

Charles scratched his head, thinking how odd that was.

Ken smiled and nodded.

"There's the light again. Seemed a bit brighter that time," Ken noticed. "You know, I don't think it's really moving, or at least it doesn't seem to be now,"

Charles replied. "Really? I thought it was moving when I saw it last time. I guess it was just an optical illusion with all the trees and darkness. It's kind of hard to tell."

"Well, it still wouldn't hurt to head toward it, whatever it is," Charles spoke as he forged forward.

They continued yelling the children's names, hoping for a reply.

⤜⤐

The kids started getting heavy eyes while they wandered through the woods.

"Come on guys. We can't slow down now," David yelled back to the others.

Sherry, Tina and Cody all tried to keep up with David as he continued walking toward the light they had been following.

Hoping that their father was somewhere near, Sherry yelled out. "Dad! Are you out here? Someone help us!" Sherry's voice sounded very tired. But still nobody answered.

"Sherry relax, we'll find our way home. I promise," stated David in a confident tone.

⤜⤐

Lilly checked on Melinda's foot and tried to make her more comfortable. "That must really hurt," Lilly said.

"Yep it's pretty sore, but it'll be fine soon I'm sure," Melinda said, sounding positive.

Lilly smiled. "So do you mind if I ask what your husband does, I mean, for a living? Charles is a banker,"

"Oh, well normally Ken writes books, but recently he's had a problem with writers block."

Lilly found it intriguing. "Wow, so Ken's a writer. How nice. Can I ask what genre of books he writes?"

"Mostly fiction or fantasy, but he has written some other books, like tips on writing and such."

"Well that's great. You're both so creative. You with your composing and Ken with his writing. I think it's great," Lilly said in a chipper voice.

"Yes, well, his writing is part of the reason we moved away from the city. Just hoping the quiet of the country might help his creativity," Melinda replied.

"I'm sure he'll do great once they get the kids back home. It's rather hard to think of book ideas when your kids are missing," Lilly said understandingly. Melinda nodded.

∽გ∾

Charles saw the light blinking up ahead of them. "There it is Ken." Charles' head dropped as he realized what it was. "All this time we were following this. I can't believe it."

Charles pointed up at a tall stick with a piece of reflective tape at the top. "Who the heck put this here?"

Ken glanced up at the shine emitting from the tape. "Maybe the kids?" Ken replied.

"Well I know Tina wouldn't have any reflective tape on her. What about your kids?" Charles questioned.

"Doubtful. So where does that leave us?" Ken inquired.

Charles scanned the dark area, not knowing which direction to go at that point. "I really don't know. All we can do is hope we run across them somewhere out here."

They continued their trek through the woods.

Chapter 11

Tina held Cody's hand as the four walked slowly through the woods.

"The light is closer now. We're almost there guys, hang in there," David said, believing his own words.

"Almost to the light, not home," Cody whispered to Tina quietly.

"Yes Cody, but I think it's a step in the right direction," Tina replied in a kind voice.

David sped up as he noticed the light looking a bit brighter. "Look, it's right up here," he shouted.

As David moved closer to the shiny object, the sudden realization of what it was kicked in.

"No!" David shrieked.

Sherry saw it too. "No, it can't be! Where is it? Where's the glowie creature?" Sherry dropped to her knees.

Tina inspected the thing which they had been following. "Why is this here?" she wondered as she looked at the tall stick.

Cody started to cry. "I wanna go home!"

"Okay look, maybe it's not the creature we saw before, but this means we aren't going in circles. We haven't seen this until now, so we haven't been here before," Tina said.

"Right, this means we have gone even *further* into the woods!" David said, having a bit of a temper tantrum.

"Not necessarily. It just means we haven't been to this exact spot, David. We could have easily missed it before. I mean look at how dark it is out here," Tina replied.

Sherry looked up at the stick in disbelief, and tried to come up with an explanation. "Maybe a hunter left it out here or something. People must hunt out here in the woods, right?"

"It's possible, but it doesn't really help," said David.

They all glanced around in the darkness looking for anything else that might help them find their way out.

Sherry started to come unglued. "Dad! Daddy! Are you out here?" She found it hard to yell as she cried out for her father in desperation.

The kids stood there in a circle, completely confused and trying to help each other to stay focused on getting out safely.

❦

Charles held his arm out in front of Ken, stopping him momentarily. "Wait. I heard something." Charles turned in circles trying to locate the direction of the sound.

"What did you hear Charles?" Ken asked.

Charles hesitated a moment and then answered. "I could've sworn I heard a child's voice."

Ken looked happy. "You did? Where was it coming from?" he asked, his voice sounding more enthusiastic than ever.

"I can't tell. It was only for a second that I heard it. I didn't have time to figure out where it was coming from."

Kens face dropped. "Well, let's just stand here for another minute, maybe you'll hear it again," he said, trying to be positive.

They stood in the dark. The wind blew through the trees, making creaking sounds. Ken had to fight off the dismay of the situation, coupled with the eerie sounds.

"There! I just heard it again!" Charles said excitedly. He pointed in the direction that he heard the voice coming from. "Come on! I know that's a child, I just know it!"

Ken and Charles walked quickly through the woods, hoping to find the children safe and sound.

⌘

Melinda nodded off on the couch from the pain medication the doctor had given her at the hospital. Lilly wandered around the Parker home, trying to stay awake in case Melinda needed anything, or the kids came back. She walked into the kitchen for a drink. She was amazed at how organized everything was.

"I should be this organized," she said to herself as she ran her finger across the sterile countertops. She walked around the quiet home and decided to play the CD that had Melinda's music. She adjusted the volume so as not to wake Melinda and took a seat in Ken's chair.

As she listened to the music, she thought back to when she and Charles were young and how much fun they had together. She giggled when she remembered the time they had gone out dancing and Charles didn't know how to dance.

"My toes are still sore," she said quietly to herself, laughing.

She silently watched over Melinda as she slept peacefully. She thought about how nice it would be to have a friend like Melinda to talk with all the time.

❧❧

Tina pulled David aside to talk to him. "David, Sherry and Cody are not doing so great. Maybe we should just stay put right here for the rest of the night."

A look of shock crossed David's face.

"Oh heck no! I didn't lug Sherry on my back for miles to give up now that she can actually walk," he said, sounding extremely annoyed.

Tina glanced back at Sherry and Cody. "I don't know, David. Cody is about to pass out and Sherry is an emotional mess, which is something I never thought I would say about her."

David looked at his brother and sister. "Ugh, I guess we can try, but it's going to be miserable. We don't have any blankets or anything soft to lay on."

"I know, but it's pretty dry right here and if we all go to sleep, before we know it, the sun will be up and it won't be so hard to find our way out."

Tina sat on the ground and bunched up some leaves to put under her head.

Sherry walked over to Tina, her face sad and tired.

"Can I lay down by you?" she asked.

Tina patted the ground next to her. "Sure, Sis, pull up a pile of leaves and make yourself at home," she quipped.

Sherry tried to giggle, but didn't have the energy.

Cody piled up leaves next to Sherry and laid his head down. Within minutes, he was fast asleep. David joined the others reluctantly.

Chapter 12

Charles and Ken walked in the direction that the voice came from.

"I know I heard a child Ken, I know I did," Charles said as he walked.

"It may have been some sort of animal Charles," Ken said, adding his two cents.

"No, it wasn't an animal. It sounded like words or something. But it was so far off I couldn't tell what the words were."

"I'm not saying it definitely wasn't a voice Charles, I'm just saying...." Charles cut Ken off.

"No, it was a child and *there* they are!" Charles dashed toward the pile of children as fast as he could, his feet getting caught up in vines as he ran.

"Tina!" he yelled out to his daughter as he approached them. Ken's legs weakened as he ran, thinking it was a dream.

"Sherry? Cody? David?" he yelled to his children in hopes that they were okay.

Charles bent over and picked up Tina. She woke up to her father shedding tears onto her face.

"Daddy?" she said in a sleepy voice. "Am I dreaming?"

Charles laughed when he heard his daughter's voice. "No honey, you aren't dreaming. I'm really here." Charles smiled.

Ken woke his children and gave them a group hug. "Oh thank God you're all right. I was so worried about you guys!" Kens voice cracked as he tried to hold back the tears.

"Daddy!" yelled Sherry with excitement.

"Dad? You found us! I *knew* you would!" yelled David, sounding extremely relieved.

"Can I go home and have something to eat now Daddy?" Cody asked his father. They all laughed as Charles and Ken got them all on their feet.

∽᠗᠔᠊

While Melinda slept, Lilly thought back to when she and Charles had visited the tree and how wonderful they felt that day. They had so much life to live still. She thought about the area and wondered why they heard the words.

"I just don't understand it," she thought to herself. "It was such a relaxing place when we were there." She thought the day over completely in her mind. She remembered them walking through the woods talking and then finding the tree. It was so huge. The roots at the base were big enough for young children to stand under or adults to sit under. It was so peaceful and inviting.

"It was so beautiful," she said aloud. She tapped her knee to the gentle music as she looked back into her memory. She giggled when she thought about Charles scrunching down to get under the roots with her. Then the horrifying memory of the aftermath of the carving rushed through her head.

"Willow Patch", she heard vividly in her head. She remembered the once relaxed state she was in faded as they scrambled to find the source. "What is Willow Patch?" She asked herself. She remembered how they tried to run away but the words 'Swear your Silence' stopped them in their tracks and how they carved it into the tree to appease whatever it was.

"I still don't understand why we had to do that. What were we swearing our silence about?" she asked aloud. She tried really hard to think of an explanation, anything at all that would make sense of the tree and the woods. She thought about her little Tina being out there with the Parker children, knowing how frightened they must be.

She thought back to how she felt when she and Charles were under the tree, talking, and being silly. She could still feel the sun on her face that shone through a small hole in one of the roots of the tree.

She closed her eyes and took herself back to that time and place. They were still so young and full of energy and hopes. Charles was a funny man, she remembered. He had such a great sense of humor that had since faded as he grew older.

"I miss that part of him," Lilly said as she thought about his laugh and his impish smile. She could remember him hugging her so tight under the tree that day and how safe she felt in his arms. She knew that their love would surpass anything. Their future was an untold story and she couldn't wait to see how it would read.

The Beginning

"It was such a beautiful day. I just don't understand what happened. What did we do that was so wrong? We carved our initials in the tree. That can't be it," she tried to rationalize. "People carve their initials in trees all the time when they are in love."

Lilly began to wander around the living room of the Parker home again. She remembered the voice they heard once more. 'Swear your Silence.' Why didn't Tina ever have any odd experiences in those woods all these years? She *had* to have seen that tree at some point. It's too big to miss. Why didn't she ever have to swear her silence? And if she did hear the voice asking her to do that, why hasn't she told us yet?

As Lilly paced through the quiet home, she passed by Melinda as she lay on the couch sleeping. She looked at her injured foot.

"Bless her heart. That really must hurt," she thought as she looked the bandages over carefully.

All of a sudden, Lilly was overwhelmed as she heard the words "Willow Patch" wisp through the room quietly.

"What?" she asked as she jumped back from the couch in a startled fashion.

"Willow Patch." The words were repeated by the unseen force.

Lilly stood there by Melinda as if ready to protect her from whatever might happen.

"Willow Patch," the words were heard again.

"What do you want?" Lilly asked of the voice, feeling nervous and shaken.

"Take her," the voice said in reply to Lilly.

Lilly was confused and not sure what she should do.

"Take her where? Why?" she asked quietly as she looked at Melinda.

"Willow Patch," the voice replied.

Lilly glanced around the room looking for where the voice was coming from to no avail. Knowing that the voice was the same one she and Charles had heard all those years ago, she knew she wasn't losing her mind.

She quickly tried to awaken Melinda. "Melinda. Melinda, wake up," Lilly pleaded as she gently tapped her on the arm. But Melinda wouldn't wake. Lilly tapped her again, but with more force.

"Melinda, you need to wake up. Something is going on here," Lilly said loudly to Melinda.

Lilly struggled to wake Melinda, but it was a lost cause. Lilly knew that she had no choice but to try to get Melinda into the wheelchair alone. Worrying about Melinda's state of sleep caused Lilly to panic as she tried to load Melinda's small but limp body into the wheelchair.

"Melinda if you can hear me, I am taking you somewhere," Lilly shouted to Melinda who was non-responsive.

Once Melinda was in the chair and strapped in, Lilly headed for the front door.

"Follow your heart," Lilly heard as she opened the front door.

"Follow my heart?" she asked of the voice.

Lilly shut the door behind them as she pushed Melinda through the front yard in the darkness.

"Follow my heart—okay, follow my heart," she repeated to herself wishing that Charles was by her side to help ease her state of panic. Lilly trudged through the yard towards the woods knowing that it had to be connected to the tree because the voice was the same one she heard many years prior.

"I hope I am doing the right thing. Oh Melinda, please wake up," she begged as she looked at the extreme darkness of the woods ahead of them. As she pushed the wheelchair, she could hear the voice ahead of her.

"Come to Willow Patch."

She turned her head occasionally to make sure she was going in the direction of the calm-sounding voice.

"Melinda? Melinda, honey, please wake up," she asked again, in hopes that Melinda would awaken to give her company on their journey.

"I don't even remember where that tree is," she thought, remembering it had been at least sixteen years since she and Charles had been to the tree. She tried to focus in the darkness, making sure she didn't push the wheelchair into a tree stump or anything that might hurt Melinda even more.

Although it had been a very long time since she had been in the woods, Lilly was aware of the wild animals that called the woods their home. As she slowly walked along, she spied a glimmer of light ahead.

"What is that?" she wondered.

The light seemed to move as she approached it.

"What on earth is that?" she said aloud. As she got closer, she could see that it wasn't anything that one would normally see in the woods. It was too big to be a lightning bug and it sure wasn't a flashlight.

"Charles?" she yelled out at the light, hoping to hear his voice in return. But nothing replied except the cold howl of the night wind.

Lilly tried to keep her nerves in check as she pushed Melinda forward in the wheelchair. The dirt was damp and stuck to the wheels of the chair, making it hard for Lilly to push.

"I don't know how much farther I can push this thing," she yelled to the voice in the darkness. Then she spotted a bright glow beyond a few trees. She struggled with the wheelchair to get there.

"I hope this is the right thing to do," she said to the sky. As she passed a few more trees, she was astonished. There it was: the big tree that displayed their initials for so long. The tree they avoided all those years. But it was different this time.

"Oh my word!" Lilly shouted in a shocked tone. She laid her hand on Melinda's shoulder as she gazed at the glow emitting from the tree. "What is that?" she asked as she moved a bit closer. Lilly inspected the tree, looking at it closely, but with extreme caution.

"Willow Patch," she heard coming from within the roots of the tree.

"Is that what this tree is called?" she asked the voice. "Is it called Willow Patch?" Lilly waited for an answer but didn't get a reply. "Why have you brought us here? Melinda is hurt and she isn't waking up. She needs help," Lilly said with tears and confusion in her eyes. She was overwhelmed by the glow and the voice coming from the tree.

Lilly checked on Melinda, noticing that she looked very pale and lifeless. It began to rain. Lilly grabbed hold of Melinda's body and tried to pull her out of the wheelchair in hopes of getting her under the huge roots of the tree. She struggled to lift her and was finally able to pull her to a dry spot under the roots. Lilly sat there with Melinda as the rain poured down.

"Melinda, please answer me. Please tell me you're okay," she said to her as she stroked Melinda's damp hair. Lilly cried as she looked out into the darkness, wondering if Melinda would be okay and where their families were. She curled up next to Melinda on the dry dirt under the tree, hoping and praying that the children would be found and that Melinda would soon awaken.

❀❀

Charles and Ken began their trek back through the woods with the children.

"Okay guys, please stay together and pay attention to what we say. We don't need to lose you again," Charles instructed them in a stern voice.

"We will, Dad," said Tina, happy that they were finally on their way home.

"Dad, you will never believe what we saw out here!" David shouted to his father.

"I can't imagine you seeing much of anything out here in the dark, David," Ken replied with a snicker.

David pulled a weed off his ankle as they walked along. "It was really cool Dad. It was some sort of glowing creature. I don't know what it was exactly, but it healed Sherry's leg and made my back better," David said to Ken.

"Whoa, whoa, whoa!" Ken exclaimed. "Sherry and you were hurt?" he asked while looking his kids over.

"Yeah, Sherry hurt her ankle Daddy," Cody said to his father.

"How'd you do that Sherry? And what healed you?" Ken asked his daughter.

"I tripped Daddy. It was really bad and David carried me for miles, but I'm okay now," she said as she smiled at David.

"And something healed your ankle? Am I hearing you correctly?" Ken asked as they walked in the darkness.

"Mr. Parker, it was some kind of creature. We don't know what it was, but we all saw it land on Sherry's shoulder," Tina replied, trying to explain what happened.

Charles looked at Tina. "Tina, you've all had a very long, frightening night. I'm sure whatever it was that you thought you saw was probably nothing."

"No, Daddy, it really happened. You have to believe us. If it hadn't done that to Sherry, she wouldn't be walking right now. And it was glowing, like a golden search light or something."

Ken and Charles looked at each other.

"Okay, we really need to concentrate on getting us all out of here safely, so let's forget about the whole thing until we get home, all right? It's raining hard now and the ground will be muddy and slippery," Ken warned the kids.

Charles and Ken walked the children through the woods, avoiding downed trees, stumps and other assorted dangers for hours. Charles legs began to get sore. He started limping.

"Daddy, you okay?" Tina asked him, noticing his limp.

"Oh I'm fine honey. Your old dad's bones are just fussing with him a bit," he said, joking.

"This rain is really making it hard to see at all," Ken said to Charles as he lifted Cody's tired body up to carry him.

"Yes it is," Charles replied while wiping the rain out of his eyes. The mud became thicker as they struggled to free their shoes from its grasp with each step. The relentless rain soaked their clothing making them all chilled to the bone.

"Hey, Ken, that's the stick we saw earlier with that tape on top. I say we should go a different way this time," Charles said, hoping to find a better and faster way out of the mucky woods.

"Good idea," replied Ken, veering to the left as they approached the tall stick. The group turned left at the stick and walked in an unfamiliar area. The rain was still falling in sheets as the children began to shiver and sneeze.

"Look!" Charles yelled as he found a path in the dirt.

"Nice, now all we have to do is follow it. It wouldn't be here if it didn't lead somewhere," Ken replied.

They followed the thin muddy path, moving branches and weeds out of the way. Within minutes, Ken reached the tree line.

"Here it is!" he yelled back to everyone with excitement. Ken pulled the children quickly through the edge of the woods.

"Yay!' yelled Sherry as she spied the houses in the distance. "We made it!"

Tears rolled down Charles' face and mixed with the rain as they walked toward the houses.

"This must be an old path that was grown over because it's closer to the front of your house, Ken." Charles mentioned to him, noticing it wasn't the same path that they used when they went to find the kids.

"You're right. But who cares? We finally got out of there safe," Ken said, feeling like a proud father.

❦❦

Melinda's still body laid under the roots of the tree as Lilly curled next to her for comfort.

"Please be okay Melinda," Lilly said to the woman she had befriended. "I brought you here because the voice told me to. I thought it was worth a try. I'm sorry if it only made things worse." Lilly thought she made the wrong choice by doing as she was told by the voice.

"I brought her here like you said! What else do you want from me?" she screamed out in anger at the tree. Lilly slid out from under the roots.

"What is it that you want? Why are we here? I did everything you said! Who are you?" Lilly shouted up at the huge tree, seeing that the glowing had stopped. "I swore my silence like you said! I did! But when our children disappeared, we *had* to talk about it!"

She felt silly trying to explain the extenuating circumstances to a tree. Lilly stumbled around the tree looking for the carving she had made years ago, but it was too dark.

"I just don't understand what it is you think I have done, and I don't understand why you asked me to bring Melinda here! What is it you want from me?" she asked again, then took cover under the roots to watch over Melinda.

As Lilly sat there watching her friend wither, she started crying and talking to herself. "Melinda, this is all my fault. I shouldn't have brought you here. I don't know, I guess I just thought it might help in some way. You wouldn't wake up and I knew the closest hospital was a very long way from our house. I was afraid that I wouldn't get there in time."

She paused for a moment. "Maybe I just wanted to believe that something magical out there really existed and that maybe it could help you. I've never really been one to fantasize—that was Charles when he was young. I always kept my feet firmly on the ground."

Lilly remembered back to that day. She remembered the feeling she had when she and Charles first came to the tree and how wonderfully safe she felt. She also remembered thinking that it would be a nice place to go and practice playing her cello, but after they heard the voice, she never wanted to return.

Lilly brushed the hair from Melinda's face.

"Please, whoever you are, if you can help my friend please do it. I don't know what's wrong with her and I'm really frightened. Our children and husbands have all gone missing and I feel so alone. Please help us. I promise I won't ever tell anyone," Lilly pleaded with the unknown voice.

Lilly perked up as she heard the voice.

"Willow Patch. Willow Patch."

She held onto Melinda as she listened quietly.

"Willow Patch. You have come to Willow Patch for help. Willow Patch can help if asked."

Lilly was shocked as she listened to the voice.

"You have asked for help and we will do so."

Lilly tried to crawl out from under the roots, but something unseen was blocking her way. She banged on what seemed to be an invisible wall of some sort. "What's going on?" she yelled as she banged harder and harder, feeling claustrophobic within the confines of the roots and the darkness.

Chapter 13

Charles, Ken and the children ran to their homes. Charles and Tina entered their home and ran to find Lilly.

"Lilly! We found them!" he said loudly as he walked through the home trying to find his beloved wife.

"Mom! We're home!" Tina screeched out to her mother at her own home, thinking she was panicking about them. But Lilly was nowhere to be found.

Ken and his children walked into their house and heard music playing. Ken walked over and turned it off.

"Melinda! Where are you? We found the kids!" Ken yelled to his wife. Sherry, David and Cody all sat on the couch, glancing around the room with a look of confusion.

"Where is she, Dad?" David asked.

"She has to be here somewhere. She couldn't even walk!" Ken replied.

A look of concern crossed Sherry's face.

"I'm going to call Charles and see if she's over at their house somehow," Ken told his children.

Sherry started her way up the stairs to the comfort of her bedroom.

"Charles, is Melinda over there?" Ken asked.

"No, I thought maybe Lilly was over at your house because she isn't here," Charles said with great concern.

Ken looked terrified that something happened to Melinda and that Lilly had to take her to the hospital.

"Okay look, I'm going to call the hospital and see if they showed up at the emergency room," Ken told Charles and then hung up quickly.

Sherry sat on her bed; looking at her clock, she noticed just how long they had been gone. "Man, it's almost morning," she thought. "Where could Mom be?"

Ken hung up the phone after calling the emergency room. "Well, I guess that's a good sign. Your mother isn't at the hospital," Ken said to David and Cody.

There was a knock on the door. Ken opened it to find Charles and Tina standing there looking very distraught.

"Any luck finding them?" Charles asked Ken.

"No, but that's not necessarily a bad thing. At least we know that Lilly didn't have to take Melinda to the hospital," Ken replied, looking somewhat baffled.

Sherry tried to relax, being safe at home. She lay back on her bed and breathed in the familiar smell of her bedroom. She closed her eyes to go over all that had happened that day, when her solitude was broken by the sound of her computer doing something. She opened her eyes to see that her paint program had once again opened and the picture of the tree was on her screen.

"No!" She screamed at the computer. "Not *this* again!"

Everyone in the house heard Sherry's scream and ran up the stairs to see what was going on.

"Daddy, look!" she yelled to him as he entered her room. "The tree!"

Tina walked up to the computer wondering what was happening and remembering how this had happened before.

"The tree! That's it Daddy, they're at the tree!" Tina yelled as she rushed out of the room.

"Tina!" Charles bellowed at her. "You're not going anywhere!"

David and Cody looked to each other for support.

"Dad, I think someone should go check it out. I mean, they could be there," David said.

"None of us are going back out there, David! We just got back after being out there all night looking for you guys," Ken replied in a huff.

"Sherry, were you messing with your computer when this image popped up?" Charles asked her.

"No sir. I was on my bed when it happened. And this isn't the first time this has happened. It did it once before when my Dad took my Mom to the hospital." She glanced at David.

"Yeah Mr. Brooks. I saw it. At first I thought Sherry was just messing with me, but it kept popping up over and over. It was really weird," David added.

Charles looked at Ken in disbelief.

"I remember the kids telling me about that, but I wasn't sure what to think about it," Ken remembered.

Charles looked at the screen intently. "This has to mean something. Maybe Tina is right. Maybe Melinda and Lilly are out there," Charles mumbled to Ken.

"Charles, we simply cannot take these kids back out there, and I'm not leaving them alone," Ken replied.

Charles rubbed his chin. "I hate to do this, but we need to go wake up Mrs. King and ask her to watch over the kids."

Ken nodded. "We never checked to see if they were at Mrs. King's house anyway, so that's a good idea," Ken added.

"I'll be right back," Charles said as he headed over to the old woman's house.

Ken studied the picture of the tree and the surrounding area on the computer. "This is just so odd. I don't understand what is going on with this place," he said to himself.

Charles knocked on Mrs. King's door. She answered looking dazed and confused.

"Yes Charles?" the old woman asked, holding her fuzzy robe closed.

"Mrs. King, I'm sorry to bother you at this time, but Mr. Parker and I have been out all night looking for the kids in the woods, and once we found them and came home, both of our wives were gone. Have you heard anything from them?"

Mrs. King shook her head. "No Charles, not a thing. So the kids were missing, were they? Are they all right?" she asked him with a bit of a surprised look on her face.

"They're all fine, but Ken and I need to go check if they went to the tree looking for us and we don't want to take the kids back out there. Would you mind watching them for us?" He felt bad that he had to ask the elderly woman.

"No problem at all Charles. Let me just get some warm clothes on first," she said as she quickly walked toward her bedroom.

Sherry wiped the sleep from her eyes as she gazed at the picture of the tree on her computer screen. She couldn't help but wonder if her mother and Lilly had been sucked into this whole mystery somehow. She looked at the big tree and the surrounding rocks and foliage. "It really is a beautiful place," she thought to herself.

Mrs. King exited her bedroom and followed Charles back to the Parker home.

"Ken! Mrs. King is here now. Let's get moving," Charles shouted to him. Ken gave his kids hugs and told them to be good for Mrs. King while he was gone and then ran downstairs to meet Charles.

"Okay, let's head back out," Charles said, still dripping from the rain.

"You know Charles; this has been one heck of a day. I don't think I will ever forget this as long as I live," Ken said as they trudged through the rain covered grass.

"I agree. This truly has been a strange day," Charles replied.

◈

Lilly desperately tried to break through whatever it was that was holding her and Melinda captive within the roots of the tree.

"What are you doing? Why won't you let me out?" she cried to the tree.

"Willow Patch." The words were heard by Lilly, sounding louder as they echoed within the tree.

"Please, if you can't help us, let us go!" she yelled at it frantically. Then, as if a switch had been turned on, the closed in area of the roots began to glow brightly. Lilly could feel the warmth as she held onto Melinda's hand.

༺༻

Charles and Ken returned to the tree, hoping to find their wives there.

"I don't see either of them here Charles!" Ken shouted to him. "Where are they?" Ken asked as they inspected the area.

"Lilly! Melinda!" Charles yelled out into the darkness. Ken walked around the area.

༺༻

Lilly was exhausted from banging on the invisible wall that kept and Melinda inside the roots when she saw Ken and Charles wandering around. She banged frantically on the walls and roots, hoping to get their attention.

"Charles! Ken! We're here! Help us!" she shouted, but her cries for help went unheard. "What is going on?" she screamed at the tree. She continued trying to get her husband's attention. Her arms became weary as she banged with all her might.

Charles checked every square inch around the tree for any hints or clues "We're going to have to go back to the house and see if they have shown up at home yet, now that we know they didn't come here looking for us and the kids."

Ken shook his head. "I don't know. I am so beyond confused, Charles. This whole day is really getting on my nerves," Ken said as he patted Charles on the back.

"I understand buddy. Let's go back to the house and see if somehow they are there and make sure old Mrs. King is hanging in there with the kids. They might have taken some other path out of here and we wouldn't have seen them," Charles said as he started walking back toward the tree line.

"So are you kid's hungry?" Mrs. King asked the tired children.

"No Ma'am," said David.

"I am!" yelled Cody while rubbing his stomach.

"Code man, you should be in bed sleeping," David said to his little brother.

"I'm not tired. I'm hungry," Cody replied.

Sherry laughed as she came back downstairs from her bedroom. "Cody, one of these days you're going to explode!"

"Okay, well, let me go look and see what I can put together for you little ones," Mrs. King said as she opened the refrigerator door.

Tina looked out the front window of the Parker home wondering if Ken and her father would find her mom and Melinda. "I sure hope they're okay. It's so cold and wet out," she said quietly.

"Our Dads will find them Tina. Don't worry," said Sherry.

"Hey! I see them!" Tina said happily. Then her jaw dropped. "But they don't have my mom and Melinda with them."

Sherry, David and Cody rushed to the front door.

"Where's mom?" Sherry yelled out to her father as they approached the house. Ken and Charles came inside.

"They didn't come back here?" asked Charles.

"No, Daddy!" Tina insisted.

"So what are you going to do Dad?" David questioned his father.

Ken tapped his foot impatiently while he pondered.

"Sherry, I need to use your computer. I want to see if there's a map of the woods. Maybe it'll help us find them if they did go into the woods to find all of us." Ken headed up the stairs with Sherry behind him.

"I can search it for you, Dad. I'm really good with computers," she bragged, trying to help out as much as possible. As they entered her room, the computer was already on and the picture of the tree was still on the screen.

Ken looked at the picture. As he walked closer, the reality of what he saw was too much to comprehend. Ken backed up and sat on the end of Sherry's bed.

"Dad? What's wrong?" Sherry asked in a concerned voice.

Ken couldn't speak. Tina, David, Cody and Charles walked in the room.

"Any luck on finding a map, Ken?" Charles asked.

David saw the look of terror on his father's face.

"Dad? What's wrong?"

Ken sat there on the bed just staring at Sherry's screen.

Charles looked at the screen to see what was disturbing Ken so badly. He was stunned when he saw the computer.

Sherry, Tina and David tried to get their fathers to speak as they stared at the picture on the screen: the picture of where they just were; the picture of the tree showing Lilly and Melinda beneath its roots.

Silence overcame the Parker home.

Chapter 14

The sun began to rise, lighting up the darkness of the Parker home. Birds chirped outside like they were excited about the upcoming day.

Four exhausted children lay sprawled across the living room furniture as if it weren't a school day. Their closed eyes fluttered as the brightness breeched the thin curtains of the Parker home.

"Ugh!" David fussed as he attempted to open his eyes and focus. He tried to get up, and found that his little brother, Cody, was stretched across him in the overstuffed recliner. "Cody, get up, man. I can't move," he said as he shoved Cody's thin legs over to one side.

"What time is it? Are they home yet?" David heard Tina questioning from the couch.

Sherry sat up next to Tina and rubbed her sleep-filled eyes. "What?" She said in a confused and sleepy voice. "Oh no! I'm late for school!" She glanced around the room and saw Tina, David and Cody. "Oh — that wasn't a dream, was it?" she said when her memory of the night before hit her like a ton of bricks.

"Welcome back to the real world, Sherry!" David said, looking peeved. "We can't go to school 'cuz we still don't know where Mom and Dad and the Brooks' are. Our parents will give us all excuses for school, don't worry about it."

"Well good morning children!" said Mrs. King as she walked from the kitchen to the living room. "Now I know you have a lot on your minds, but you need to eat. So, I brought you some milk and donuts." She set a tray down on the coffee table.

"Mrs. King, did any of our parents come back home yet?" Tina inquired. She picked up a donut and a glass of cold milk.

"I'm afraid I don't have any news for you children as of yet. But I wouldn't worry. I'm sure they're all fine and will be back soon." The old woman smiled and winked at Tina.

She sat in Ken's favorite chair. "Well now. Isn't this a comfy chair?"

Sherry fidgeted on the couch, knowing that it had been at least four hours since she had seen her father and Mr. Brooks.

"Guys, we need to finish eating and go out to the woods and see what's going on."

She felt her stomach turn when she thought of the night before: Mr. Brooks and her father looking at the picture of the tree, with her mother and Mrs. Brooks beneath it.

"I agree," said David. "It's been a long time since they said they were going back out to find that tree and our moms. Anything could have happened in that much time."

David stuffed one more powdered donut in his mouth. He nudged Cody who was still snoozing in the chair. "Come on Cody! If you don't get up now all the donuts will be gone," David tempted his little brother whose appetite was more like that of a lion than a small child.

"Did someone say Donuts?" Cody said, as he slowly tried to push his tired body up from the cozy chair. "Don't eat them all! I didn't get any yet!" he yelled while reaching for the tray with glazed over eyes.

Mrs. King giggled at Cody. "There's plenty more in the kitchen child." She got up to refill the tray of food.

"Thanks, Mrs. King, but we really don't have time to wait for Cody to eat a bunch of donuts. We need to get moving," said Tina as she slipped her shoes on, still mud- covered from the previous night in the woods. She thought about her mom and dad out in those woods, possibly hurt or lost. "Now I know how they felt when I was out there," she thought to herself.

"Mrs. King, can you stay here with Cody since he hasn't finished eating?" Sherry asked kindly.

"Not a problem." Mrs. King replied.

"But I want to go too!" Cody yelled as they opened the front door.

"Cody, we need you and Mrs. King here in case Mom and Dad or the Brooks' come back." She tried to make it sound like a mission so he would stay behind, knowing it may not be safe.

Cody sat on the couch, two mini donuts in each hand. "Okay, but I get to go with you next time," he proclaimed. Sherry shot her little brother a wink as she closed the door.

The air was refreshing, but none of them could enjoy it knowing that their parents were missing. What would have been an excellent day to play outside was going to be anything but that.

"Okay, obviously the first place we have to check is back at the tree. It's daytime, so we should be reasonably safe," Tina said to Sherry and David.

They walked the familiar path toward what used to be Tina's sanctuary, her quiet reading spot. The foliage in the woods was all covered with morning dew, making wet stains on the children's clothing as they walked.

"David, do you think Mom and Dad are okay?" Sherry whispered to her brother as they walked.

David whispered back. "I can't say for sure, but let's think positive, okay? The thought of them being hurt makes me feel horrible for getting them involved in all of this."

Tina kept trudging toward the tree, hoping that she'd find at least one of their parents by the tree for whatever reason. She could hear Sherry and David whispering behind her. She couldn't understand what they were saying, but she knew it wasn't her business anyway. "Okay guys, almost there. Let's make sure we stick together. No splitting up and going separate ways," she said sternly. David and Sherry nodded their heads.

As they approached the huge tree, they noticed a strange sound. A sound they had never heard in their prior trips to the tree.

"What is that? It sounds like..." said Tina.

Sherry and David looked at each other and then at Tina. They all stood very still and listened closely. Tina moved her head back and forth, trying to pinpoint exactly where the sound was coming from. David took a step closer in the direction of the tree root cover that they all once sat under.

"Here! It's coming from here! I can hear it!" David yelled to the girls as he motioned for them to join him. The girls leaned in toward the tree roots.

"Sherry, do you hear that?" Tina asked her.

Sherry's eyebrows furrowed as she listened closely, trying to identify what it was. Sherry tried to go under the roots to listen, but wasn't able to.

"Ouch!" she yelped. "I just hit my head on something. Am I bleeding?" she asked her brother.

"Nah, but what did you hit your head on?" David asked.

"I guess I didn't duck down far enough when I went to sit under the roots." She rubbed her forehead a bit and tried again, this time, being more careful. She put her hand out in front of her to make sure she didn't do it again and was stunned when she noticed her hand was being stopped by something she couldn't see.

"What the...?" Sherry was boggled. She rubbed her hand across what seemed to be glass. But it couldn't be glass. Even the cleanest glass has a spot or fingerprint somewhere on it. Sherry reasoned with herself. "David! Tina!" she yelled. "This wasn't here before."

She took one of each of their hands and pushed them against the invisible object.

"Whoa—what the heck is going on Tina?" David asked, looking incredibly mystified and a bit frightened.

Tina slowly inspected the smooth surface of the invisible barrier covering her reading spot. "Okay, this has never happened before, I can guarantee you that!"

They all decided to put their ears against the barrier, hoping to clearly hear the sound they heard before.

Sherry stepped back from the barrier. "Okay, that's just creepy! It's like a bunch of mumbling or something." She shook her head in confusion and fear.

"David, do you hear mumbling too?" asked Tina.

"Yeah, it's like if someone was buried alive and you had your ear to the ground on their grave."

David stepped back where Sherry was standing. Tina turned and faced them.

"Okay, we have to be rational about this. I know this has been a really weird couple of days, but if we start freaking out we aren't going to be of any help to any of our parents."

"True. But how do we know what that is in there? I mean, it could be really dangerous to mess with," said David.

"I agree with David. For all we know our parents are in there and they could be hurt or something," said Sherry, shivering at the thought.

They all stood and stared at the bizarre force field in bewilderment.

"Okay look, I think we need to go talk to Mrs. King. She's lived here her whole life and she's old. I mean, maybe she has some ideas or something." Tina thought back to when the old woman told her the story of when she got lost in the woods as a child.

David shook his head. "I personally think we need to call the police. I mean, we're not talking about a lost cat or something. Our parents are gone and this whole bit with the creepy tree. Seriously, we can't possibly handle this on our own anymore." He snapped a twig that he pulled off the tree. Tina and Sherry looked at David like he had lost his mind.

"Let's take a vote," Tina said loudly. "All in favor of calling the police, raise your hand."

David popped his hand up as high as he could.

"All in favor of talking to Mrs. King, raise your hand." Sherry and Tina raised their hands. Tina smiled at David. "Sorry David but majority rules, two to one in favor of Mrs. King."

Sherry and Tina turned and began walking back to the Parker home. As they cleared the tree line, Tina noticed the house next to the Parkers had its curtains open.

"Wow, I don't think I have ever seen the curtains open in any of the houses on this street except ours, Mrs. Kings and of course yours," she said to Sherry. "In fact, all three of the houses in between Mrs. Kings and your house have their curtains open."

As they got closer to the street, Tina saw the faces of the elderly people that lived in the homes. "Uhm, guys? They're all watching us," Tina said in a shaky voice. She looked back at an old man in one of the homes. He stared back with an intense look of curiosity. Sherry glanced at each of the houses. "Okay, creepy!" she said back to Tina as they approached the Parker home.

The Beginning

Cody stood hopefully in the front yard of his house waiting for Sherry, David and Tina to return with his parents. He saw them exit the woods, but they were alone.

"Cody, you really need to stay in the house with Mrs. King. She's getting way too old to chase after you," Sherry shouted.

The kids entered the Parker home. Mrs. King was sitting in Ken's reading chair. "Well that was certainly a quick trip," Mrs. King said as the kids walked in the door. "I guess you didn't have any luck finding your parents?" she asked of them.

Chapter 15

Tina sat on the couch along with David and Sherry.

"Mrs. King, remember how you told me the story of how you got lost in the woods when you were young?" Tina said, wiping the sweat from her brow.

"Yes dear, I remember," replied Mrs. King.

"Can you remember anything else about the woods or the tree? Anything you may have forgotten to tell me? I know it was a long time ago, but since you are the only person left that has had an odd experience out there in the woods, I thought you could help," Tina said to the kind woman.

"I'm sorry Tina, but I told you everything I had to tell. That's all I can remember and my mind isn't what it used to be I'm afraid," she said, looking sad. "What about any of the neighbors? The people in the other three houses on this street? Have you met any of them? Because I haven't and I have been here my entire life."

It started to dawn on Tina how very odd it was that she had never seen any of them in their yards or going anywhere. Only Mrs. King had seemed to live a normal life on their street. That was besides the Brooks family and the Parkers.

"Well now, it's been quite a while since I have seen any of them. At least since all their children grew up and moved out. They're all old like me now. Probably just don't have much energy left for gallivantin' about these days."

Tina tried to absorb all the information that Mrs. King had to offer. "The reason I was asking you about them was because I have never personally met or seen any of them until today. On our way back from the woods, they all had their curtains open and they were staring at us. It was kind of freaky to tell you the truth," Tina said as she calmed the goose bumps on her arms.

Mrs. King raised an eyebrow. "I can imagine that it seemed strange to you and your friends Tina, but I am quite sure it was no more than coincidence. When you get to be our age, being nosey is just about all you can do for entertainment!" She brushed a piece of lint off her dress.

"That's okay Mrs. King. We understand. We just thought maybe…" Tina glanced at David knowing that he still wanted to involve the police. Tina crossed her arms. "I just don't know what to do or what is going on. I'm so confused. All this weird stuff happening, and all of it appears to be related to a tree that I have been reading under for years. I just don't get it."

Mrs. King adjusted herself in the chair. "Don't be alarmed when I ask this but have you tried calling the hospital? It is a possibility that they are there."

Sherry's face dropped at the thought of her parents being hurt in any way. She was already concerned about the injury her mother had gotten the day before.

"What time is it now?" David inquired.

"It's almost noon dear," replied Mrs. King.

"We need to figure out where our parents are *now* guys. Let's get moving."

They began the long trudge back out to the woods.

"I feel so gross. We didn't even wash up after being in the woods all night," Sherry said as she tried to brush crud off her pants.

"Who are you worried about seeing you out here Sherry? The animals? Or maybe that weird flying thing that healed us last night?" David asked his sister, sounding annoyed.

"Geez, someone is in a rotten mood," Sherry muttered under her breath.

"Of course I'm in a rotten mood! And you should be, too Sherry!" David yanked a leaf off of a tree that they passed by.

"Okay you two, try to remember what we're here for and try not to get on each other's nerves," Tina said trying to stifle the argument.

Sherry and David glared at each other in silence. They walked the familiar path back to the tree, only this time not with the same giddiness they went there with the very first time. When they finally arrived at the tree, they all looked around for their parents once again.

"See! They still aren't here girls!" David said snidely.

Tina walked over to the roots and felt for the barrier they found earlier. She closed her eyes to depend on her hearing alone to understand what was happening.

David and Sherry watched Tina quietly, not sure what she was doing. They saw her nod her head slightly.

Both of her hands were on the invisible barrier. She pressed her forehead to the wall and seemed to be in a meditative state. David and Sherry started to get a bit concerned.

"Tina? You okay?" Sherry asked her best friend. Tina didn't answer.

David took a step closer to Tina. "Hey. Tina? Don't bug out on us now," David said, trying to make her giggle or something. Nothing David did or said worked. She wouldn't budge. She appeared to be frozen in time.

Sherry and David walked around to the other side of the roots where the barrier continued. They peered through to the other side and saw Tina standing there.

"Hey Tina! Pantomime isn't your thing!" Sherry gibed when she saw her friend holding her hands up in the air as if something was actually there. But still, there was no answer from Tina. Sherry's smile from the silly joke quickly turned into a frown. She was really worried about Tina. She was usually the most serious of them all.

Tina seemed to come to as she took a few steps backward. David and Sherry ran back to the other side of the roots.

"Tina!" Sherry cried out to her. What happened? What were you doing? We were talking to you and you wouldn't answer us!" Sherry hugged Tina.

David looked into Tina's tear-filled eyes. "Hey girl, you okay? We were starting to think you were becoming part of the tree for a while there."

Tina shook her head a bit and looked at David. "I — I'm okay, but I need to tell you something." She sat on the ground. David and Sherry joined her.

"So what's up?" David quickly questioned her.

Tina glanced around the area looking rather frightened. "Promise me you won't think I'm insane, please!" Tina pleaded with her friends.

David laughed. "After all the things that have happened since we moved here, I doubt there is anything you could say to make me think you're crazy."

David patted Tina on the hand. Tina took a deep cleansing breath.

"Okay, here we go. This whole tree thing and all the weird stuff that's been happening—it goes way deeper than that. And I mean *way* deeper." She looked to them, hoping not to get laughed at.

"What do you mean by 'deep' Tina?" Sherry asked.

"Okay look, when I put my hands on the barrier at the roots, I felt a pull on me like it was controlling me in some way. My head was pushed toward it like someone had their hand on the back of my head, shoving me into it. And I couldn't talk, I heard you for a while and then all I could hear was this creepy voice. Not the one we hear all the time. This one was different. It sounded like it detested me. I've never felt anything like that before. It was really frightening." Tina shivered at the thought of the voice.

"What did the voice say?" David asked, assuming she couldn't remember the whole event that just took place.

"I remember every word David. That's what is so scary. This thing or person or whatever is holding our parents captive," she said, as her tears dripped onto the dry ground from her cheeks.

"What? All of them?" David asked in a shocked tone.

"Yes David, all of them. It told me that if I didn't bring the queen back, we would never see our parents again," Tina said, her arms wrapped around her knees.

Sherry stood up and her temper took over. "Well I'm not letting any creepy thing hurt our parents!"

David jumped up as well. "Sherry, how do we fight against something we can't see or hear? Only Tina heard that voice."

Tina pushed herself up from the ground, her legs were shaking. "I know how to get our parents back, but I don't want to have to do it," she said.

"Okay, then tell us so we can get our parents back. Where's this queen at and what does she or it look like?" David tried to be in control again.

"David, you don't understand. Neither one of you do. It's not that simple." Tina explained.

"What's wrong Tina?" Sherry asked, sensing she was hiding something.

"Believe me Sherry, I want my parents back too, but I don't think I can do this."

Chapter 16

Tina walked out of the woods with her head down.

"Wait a minute Tina! You can't just give up like that!" David yelled at Tina as he followed her reluctantly.

Tina took off running back to her home. David and Sherry tried to keep up to get some answers. Tina swung her front door open and ran up to the comfort of her bedroom. She jumped onto her purple bed and looked up at her Harry Potter poster on the ceiling.

"You'd be able to do it, wouldn't you Harry?" she said in a sad voice. Tina thought about how she always envied people that were involved in something mysterious like Harry Potter always was. She started feeling as if she finally got what she always wanted, but couldn't handle it once she was put to the test. She didn't really have what it took to be a true adventurist. She rolled over and cried silently into her pillow.

"Tina! Tina are you up there?" Sherry shouted through the house. David followed his sister since he was unfamiliar with Tina's home.

Tina pulled her head away from her pillow. "I'm up here," she murmured quietly as she sobbed.

Sherry and David entered her room.

"Tina, look, I'm sorry if I upset you. I'm just so worried about our folks. If there is anything we can do to set them free, we need to do it, don't we?" Sherry asked in a calm tone.

Tina rolled over. Her pillow was soaked with tears. "I want my parents back so bad Sherry. You have to believe me. And I know you want yours back too, but this—this thing that spoke to me. It was evil. I could feel it in my soul. It hated me and probably hates you and our parents too," she closed her eyes and tried to forget how it made her feel.

❧❧

Mrs. King sat in the Parker's living room and sewed while Cody played with his trucks in the middle of the floor.

"Blam! Bang! My truck is bigger than yours monster man!" Cody yelled as he plunged the trucks together, in his imaginary world of make believe.

"You have quite an imagination there little guy," Mrs. King said to Cody.

"I love playing with my trucks. When I grow up I want to drive one!"

She stood up. "Well now that sounds like a fine job Cody. Now if you'll behave for a moment, I need to get a fresh cup of tea." She slowly walked into the kitchen. She reached for the teapot that sat so neatly on Melinda's stovetop.

"Oh my!" Mrs. King reached for a kitchen chair and sat down. Cody heard her and went to the kitchen to check on his elderly babysitter. He saw her slumped over in the chair. A groaning sound came from the woman that frightened little Cody, but he checked on her anyway.

"Mrs. King. Are you okay?" He hesitantly asked her. Mrs. King sat up straight and looked into Cody's eyes. "Don't worry Cody. I'll be fine. I have spells like this every now and again." He smiled and went back to playing.

David and Sherry sat on Tina's bed and tried to talk about what happened at the tree.

"Do you guys believe in immortals?" Tina asked her friends.

"You mean like Apollo?" I had to do a report about him in school once," Sherry spoke up.

"Yeah, I've read a lot about them in school too," said David.

Tina hung her head. "Yes, but do you believe in them?" she asked once more.

"Well, I don't know. I mean, I suppose they could," David said quietly as if he was embarrassed to admit that he might believe in immortals.

"David. They *do* exist!" Tina barked at him. "They're everywhere and they have descendants all over the world." Tina tried to get David to understand that she wasn't playing around. "The thing that has our parents, it didn't just speak to me David. It showed me things from long ago that I couldn't possibly know. Horrible wars going on between all of the immortals. So much pain, but none of them could die because they were in fact immortal. Just like in our world, there is a balance of good and evil, it's the same in the immortal world." Tina stood up and paced across her floor.

"So you're telling us that the thing that spoke to you was an immortal? Like for real?" Sherry questioned.

"Yes, I am assuming, Sherry. Otherwise it wouldn't have known about all the wars."

"But what does all of that have to do with our parents and the tree?" David was beyond confused but ready to do whatever it took to get his parents back.

"Sherry, go get my pad of paper out of my drawer over there," Tina instructed her.

Sherry rushed to find the purple pad of paper.

"Okay, these are the facts," Tina said. "I have been going to that same tree since I was very young and nothing strange or bad ever happened in all those years. I felt, if anything, very comfortable when I was there. When you guys moved in and we came out to the tree, odd things started happening. Not bad, just odd. We all heard whispering in the wind. We know now that it was saying Willow Patch. There was writing on the tree that David and Cody saw, and when Sherry and I went to see it, it wasn't there.

"Then there are the pictures and drawings. Those alone were weird. Then the story Mrs. King told me about when she was little and got lost in the woods. All of our parents disappear, and now we have an evil immortal that wants his queen back in exchange for our parents." Sherry finished writing all the facts down.

"This is nuts. How are we ever going to find this 'queen'? I mean, there are only six houses on this street and no other houses for at least fifteen miles!" Sherry was uneasy thinking about the task at hand.

David stood up. "Okay you two, chill out or we won't ever find her. We need to think positive and remember one *huge* thing. If some horrible creature got hold of one of us, our parents would do everything and anything to save us!" He puffed out his chest.

Tina decided to tell her friends everything about her experience. Even the things she didn't want to know herself.

"David, there's something else I need to tell you. I should have told you before, but it was really upsetting to even think about. When it was showing me all the wars between the immortals, it also showed me at the tree when I was a little girl; the first time I went to the woods and found the tree."

"Yeah? What did you see?" David asked.

Tina's throat tightened a bit. "I didn't know this happened, I didn't remember. Believe me, if I did I would have told you guys before now."

"Well, what is it?" Sherry asked.

"Apparently when I went to the tree the first time, something odd did happen. When I sat under its roots, the tree lit up like a Christmas tree. There was light everywhere, but it was for a very short time. I honestly don't remember that happening, but it was one of the visions that the immortal showed me."

"Wow! So you *did* have a weird experience with the tree before we came here. You just didn't remember it!" Sherry shrieked. "That is *so* cool!"

Tina walked in circles. "Yeah but I don't know why I didn't remember it and still don't. I mean, how could I have *not* seen something like that going on when I was there? It's creeping me out."

"I don't know Tina, but it might help us in some way just knowing that it happened," David said.

❧❧

Cody brought a glass of water to Mrs. King as she sat at the Parker home kitchen table.

"Here Mrs. King. Drink a glass of water. Mommy says water is really good for you." Cody smiled at her.

She took the glass and drank a few sips. "Thank you Cody. You have a very kind heart. Did you know that?" she said with a smile.

"My whole body is kind Mrs. King," Cody said pointing to himself from head to toe.

"Land sakes child, you are a funny one!" Mrs. King said as she chuckled.

"Are you feeling better now? he asked her.

"Yes dear. I'm feeling much better now. Thank you for the glass of water," she said as she placed the glass on the table. "You know Cody, they say that acts of kindness to others in the world are counted, and the people are rewarded for them."

She winked at Cody. Cody smiled.

"Really? I do a lot of things for my mom and dad. Sometimes I sweep the kitchen floor with Mom when she lets me. And Dad lets me help him in the yard. I rake the leaves," he said with a big grin.

"Well then, it sounds like you have earned many rewards," she said to Cody.

"When do I get my rewards?" he asked her.

"Oh now, none of us really know when our reward will come to us, but rest assured you will be rewarded at some point in your life. That's why it's so important to always be good and try to help others."

Chapter 17

Tina looked at her reflection in the bedroom mirror. She thought to herself. "Why did that happen? Why only with me? That tree has never lit up like that before."

She looked at herself, thinking she wasn't anyone special.

"Man, when I think of the possibilities now. I mean, why would the tree do that when you were there, Tina? Maybe you were someone really cool in a past life!" Sherry declared excitedly.

"I don't believe in past lives Sherry. Besides, if I was someone really cool before, don't you think I'd still have part of that 'coolness' in *this* life? Believe me, I'm nothing special. I'm just a normal girl like you," Tina scoffed.

"Hey now!" Sherry said with her eyebrows furrowed. "You make me sound like I'm just some boring girl. I like to think I am special in my own ways." She looked in the mirror and ran her fingers through her red hair.

David chuckled. "Oh yeah Sherry, you're special all right. You were made specially to be a pain in my..."

"David!" Tina cut him off. "Be nice!" she said to him. "I think we should go back over to your house and check on Cody. Mrs. King is probably worn out by now."

She walked out of her bedroom and headed downstairs. They walked toward the Parker home. As they passed Mrs. Kings house, Tina looked at the pole that held the Hummingbird feeder during the summer months. "Man I miss the simple days," she said to herself.

"Uhm Tina? Look!" Sherry said, interrupting her calming memories.

"What, Sherry?" Sherry pointed at the house next to Mrs. King's. Inside of the front window, an elderly woman stood watching them. She stared at them as they passed by, making them feel very uncomfortable.

"Geez, take a picture why don't ya?" David said snidely.

They passed the next house. Another elderly woman stared at the children as they walked by.

"What's with these people all staring at us like we're aliens or something?" David asked Tina and Sherry.

"I don't know. I never see any of them. They're always closed up in their houses. I have to admit that it is very strange that all of a sudden they open their curtains and happen to be watching us every time we're outside," Tina answered.

They passed the house right before the Parker home where an old man glared at them intensely as if he truly hated them.

"Really nice people around here, huh Tina?" David said. "No wonder you were so happy when we moved in!" He chuckled.

They entered the Parker home and saw Cody sitting on the kitchen floor. "What's up Code?" Sherry asked her little brother.

"Oh I'm just doing good things for Mrs. King so I get lots of rewards later. She wasn't feeling good before and I got her a glass of water," He chimed with a smile. They looked at Mrs. King.

"You okay Mrs. King? Cody didn't wear you out did he?" David asked.

"Oh no. He's a sweet one. I just had a bit of a spell. Nothing to worry yourselves about. He was a big help and got me a glass of water," she said, winking at Cody.

"That was very nice of you Cody. You sure are growing up fast!" Sherry admitted.

Tina noticed that Mrs. King's breathing was erratic. She worried about her old friend, but knew she had a mind of her own.

"Mrs. King, why don't we go sit down in the living room where you can be more comfortable?" Tina asked her, hoping she'd agree.

Mrs. King stood up from the kitchen chair and slowly made her way to the comfort of the living room couch. Tina, Sherry and David sat down and prepared to tell Mrs. King the news about Tina's experience at the tree. They all hoped she might have some ideas about what was going on, even though her memory wasn't serving her as well as it used to.

"Mrs. King, I don't want to keep bothering you with all this tree stuff; I know you're not feeling well. If I could just tell you one more thing and get some feedback, it would be great," Tina said shyly. Mrs. King looked pale and exhausted. "Well, the thing is that something really frightening happened when we went back to look for our parents."

David cracked his knuckles. Sherry elbowed him to keep him quiet.

"Tina, I've known you since you were the size of one of my garden gnomes and if I can help you in any way, you know I will." She grinned at Tina.

"Okay, well when we went out there to find our parents the first time today, we tried to go under the roots of the tree, but there was some kind of invisible barrier there. Then we came back here to talk to you, and thought you might have some other information that would shed some light on it all, but you didn't.

Then we went back to check it out again, see if anything changed. The barrier was still there and when I put my hands against it, it seemed to take over my body and I heard talking and it was really scary," Tina said, hoping Mrs. King believed her.

"An invisible barrier you say? Now there's something you don't see every day," Mrs. King said jokingly to the kids.

"I'm serious Mrs. King. Even Sherry and David could hear mumbling coming from the barrier the first time we went out there." Tina tried hard to stress the truth of the matter.

"Oh now, don't get upset Tina sweetie. I was just playing around with you," the old woman replied.

"Anyway, the voice said something to me Mrs. King. It sounded very scary. It made me see visions of immortals, good ones and evil ones — at war. Then it showed me a vision of me as a small child at the tree and it was all lit up really bright. I don't remember the tree ever doing anything like that. It told me that I have to bring the queen back to it or we will never see our parents again! Mrs. King I'm really scared!" Tina said with tears in her eyes.

"There's a scary man in the tree?" Cody asked, with a look of terror on his face. Sherry hugged her little brother.

"It's okay Cody. You don't ever have to go back out there again."

"Yeah Cody. Don't worry. We'll handle it and bring Mom and Dad back. Just think about happy stuff okay?" David said in a sweet voice. Tina felt bad for scaring Cody.

"So, this voice said what about a queen?" Mrs. King asked.

"It said to bring the queen back. I'm assuming she's an immortal like the ones I saw in the vision, but I have no idea where she would be. I'm just a kid. How would I be able to search all over the world for a missing queen?" Tina said looking more confused than ever.

"Immortals huh?" Mrs. King uttered, sounding like she didn't believe her, but wanted to so badly. "Dear, all I can tell you is to follow your heart. My late husband always said that to me. He was a good man, God rest his soul." She bowed her head.

"Follow my heart? Mrs. King, I think my heart is just as confused as my brain," Tina quipped.

"There might be something to that Tina," David said.

"How is that David?" asked Sherry.

"Well, you said that in the vision you saw yourself at the tree and it was glowing, right?" Tina nodded her head. David continued. "Well maybe it was doing that for a reason. Maybe you are part of this whole thing. I mean, you *are* the only one that the immortal, or whatever it is, spoke to. It didn't talk to me or Sherry and we touched the barrier too. We only heard muffled mumbling. Just think about it Tina. Why is it that you were able to draw a picture of the tree on Sherry's computer *and* at home with colored pencils and yet both came out looking like photographs?" David stared Tina in the eyes.

"You have got to be kidding me David. There is *no* way I'm involved. I mean sure, some weird stuff has happened to me, but I'm not like thousands of years old! I'm not an immortal and my life is so completely boring most of the time. Nothing even remotely exciting ever happens to me. Well, at least not until you guys moved here." Tina insisted.

Mrs. King coughed into her hands. "Tina, we all have a purpose in this world. I don't know exactly what yours is but I'm sure you have one," said Tina's old neighbor.

Tina turned her back to Mrs. King. "I am not believing this. Nope. It can't be. I'm just a kid," she said shaking her head.

"And I am but an old woman, but we all have purpose in our lives Tina and we have to accept it," Mrs. King replied to her stubborn young friend.

"Look everyone, I know this is crazy, but our parents are still being held captive by that—that thing out there in the woods. We can't just sit around arguing. We need to figure out where the queen is," David said loudly.

"I say we go talk to some of those nosey neighbors that have had their curtains open lately. I mean, none of us have met them except Mrs. King," Sherry chimed in.

"What are their names?" David asked Mrs. King.

"Let's see. There's the Talbots. They're in the house right next to me. That's where my late husband grew up. Mr. Talbot passed on in the late 1970's. Then next to Mrs. Talbot is Mrs. Franklin. She was widowed before I was. Then right here next to your house, David, is Mr. Pendleton. His wife left him many years ago. Serves him right, the old grouch!" Mrs. King expressed her dislike of the old man.

The kids absorb everything she said, wishing they had brought Tina's purple pad of paper with them. Tina looked a bit disturbed. "Mrs. King. You said the people next to you were the Talbots?" she questioned.

"Yes dear. Very nice people," she replied.

"And you said your husband grew up there?" Tina asked again.

"Yes. They raised him well."

Tina tapped her chin. "Then why was your husband's last name "King" instead of "Talbot?" Tina asked.

"Oh, that's right. You didn't know that. The Talbots adopted him when he was very young. But when he became a man, he changed his last name to King," she answered quickly.

Tina nodded her head. "Well that solved that mystery. Now, if I could get my head on straight and figure out the rest."

The kids left Cody once again with Mrs. King and headed out to Mr. Pendleton's house.

"Old Mr. Pendleton better not be grouchy today! I'm in no mood to deal with that!" said Tina in an unseemly loud tone.

They walked up the cobblestone path leading to his front door. Weeds had worked hard to take over his yard. They approached the door and knocked. They heard scuffling about inside the home. The door opened slightly.

"What do you kids want? I'm not buying any candy bars or cookies!" he barked at them. The kids looked at each other and David snickered.

"Uhm sir. Is your name Mr. Pendleton?" Tina asked the old crouched over man.

"Yeah, and what do you want? I have work I have to finish up."

"Well sir, we were wondering if you had noticed anything strange going on in this area." Tina said in a timid voice.

"I don't know nothin' about nothin'! Now go on you kids! Off my property!" the old man yelled like he was talking to a pack of wild dogs.

David couldn't stop laughing at the old man. "Geez, he's a fun guy isn't he?" David kidded.

"More like a 'fun-gus'," Sherry added to the joke.

"Gosh, now I'm kind of glad I never met some of these other people," said Tina as she rolled her eyes.

"Well, we still have two more houses to go to," said Sherry.

They walked up to Mrs. Franklin's home. On the porch was a tattered rug that read "Home Sweet Home". They knocked on the door. They didn't hear anything at all. They knocked again.

"I guess she's either gone or asleep. We can come back later," said Sherry.

They headed to the last house where Mrs. King's late husband grew up years ago. The Talbot home. They knocked on the door. The elderly woman that watched them walk down the street earlier answered the door.

"Can I help you?" she asked the kids.

"Ma'am, we were just wondering if you had ever heard of anything strange going on in the area." Tina hoped for better results than they had with Mr. Pendleton.

"Strange? What do you mean by strange?" The woman glared at them.

"Well, anything about a tree that was different. Or maybe voices that seem to come from nowhere?"

The old woman slammed the door immediately. As the kids gave up and started walking back out to the sidewalk, they noticed Mrs. Talbot in her front window as she yanked her curtains shut.

"Darn, I guess we ticked her off." David said.

They walked down the street toward the Parker home feeling as if they had gained no ground at all.

"How are we ever going to figure this out guys? The neighbors that are home won't talk to us and Mrs. King has no idea. Worst of all, our parents' lives are at stake and we are the only ones that can help them," Sherry said, sounding panicked.

David opened the front door of his house and Tina and Sherry followed him.

"Mrs. King?" David yelled as they entered the living room. Mrs. King was lying on the couch. Tina looked concerned.

"Are you alright Mrs. King?" she asked as she kneeled down on the floor next to the couch.

"Tina, you worry too much child," the old woman said.

"Cody!" Sherry yelled for her brother, who ran down the stairs with one hand holding a truck and the other holding the banister.

"What?" shouted Cody.

"Have you been causing any trouble for Mrs. King? She looks worn out," Sherry questioned her brother.

"No. I was just in my room playing with my trucks," he replied in honesty.

Mrs. King looked haggard and ready to go to sleep for the day. Her breathing was still a bit erratic.

"Mrs. King, maybe you should drive yourself to the hospital and get checked, just to be on the safe side," Tina said to her.

Mrs. King replied, "Tina, if I leave, David would have to stay here and watch Cody, and I know you don't want that. Not only that, but you would have no choice but to call the police for help. You girls don't need to be running around the woods without a strong boy with you for protection."

David smiled and puffed his chest out again. "She's right you know. You girls would be sunk if one of you tripped again and I wasn't there to carry you."

Mrs. King sat up a bit on the couch. "Did you have any luck with the other neighbors?" She cleared her throat.

"Actually, no. Mr. Pendleton was mean and said he doesn't know anything about anything." Sherry answered.

David chuckled. "No, what he said was 'I don't know nothin' about nothin'!"

"And Mrs. Franklin?" asked Mrs. King.

"She wasn't home, or was asleep," replied Sherry.

"And Mrs. Talbot slammed the door in our faces and shut her curtains," said Tina.

"Well then I guess I wasn't of much help was I?" Mrs. King said.

Tina kissed Mrs. Kings forehead. "Mrs. King, you're a *huge* help to us. You watched Cody all this time and at least we have the names of all the neighbors. Hopefully Mrs. Franklin will answer her door soon," said Tina with a positive attitude.

"So what can we do now guys?" asked Sherry.

"Let's go in the kitchen and grab a few sandwiches and head back out to the tree," Tina responded.

"Oh not the tree again!" snipped Sherry.

"Well, it's the only place where we seem to get any kind of answers, guys. I don't like the thought of going back any more than you do, but we have to," Tina said as she and Sherry grabbed the bread and lunchmeat. They threw together some sandwiches and each took one to eat on the way back to the tree.

"I can tell you guys this much, I'm *not* touching that tree!" said David sternly.

Sherry looked at her brother. "What a chicken!"

"I am not! I've been taking care of you girls this whole time haven't I? I just don't want what happened to Tina to happen to me, that's all," David stated.

"Don't worry David. Nobody is asking you to touch the tree," said Sherry.

They munched away at their sandwiches as they trudged through the bushes.

"Man! That tasted like more!" David said as he brushed the bread crumbs off his lips. Tina giggled at David.

They started to feel tense as they got closer to what used to be Tina's favorite place in the world.

"Is it just me or does it feel really uncomfortable around here now?" Sherry observed.

David rubbed his arms. "Yeah it doesn't feel right at all."

Tina looked at the roots that she was practically glued to the last time they were there. "Okay guys, we have about five hours before it gets dark, so we need to figure this out soon," Tina said trying to keep her wits about her.

David wandered around the tree, passing the big boulder that was close by. "What is this?" David asked as he stopped walking. Sherry and Tina joined him. All of them inspected the boulder, completely astonished at what they saw. Sherry ran her fingertips across the etching that was never there before.

"First the tree, now the boulder? What the heck is going on?" Sherry yelled to the sky.

David and Tina looked at the etching. It looked as if someone had taken a very sharp tool and scratched a drawing into the side of the huge stone.

"Did either one of you look at this when we were here earlier today?" Tina asked David and Sherry. They shook their heads negatively.

"Man, I had enough trouble trying to put all the other pieces of this mess together and now there's another piece! I'm *not* a detective! I'm just a kid! We're *all* just kids!" Tina became angry as she tried to reason with whatever forces were causing all the problems. "What's this drawing about?"

Tina turned away and walked over to the tree. David looked closely at the new clue, trying to make sense of it.

"Hey Tina, Sherry? Come here a second," David instructed them. He pointed to the drawing. "Look at this. It looks like a map of the woods and it even shows the houses on our street."

"How is that a map?" Sherry asked, not really seeing what David was seeing.

"Okay, see this area right here? That's the big tree. I know because it shows this boulder right next to it. It's a rather primitive looking map, but it *is* a map."

Sherry and Tina looked closer. "Oh yeah! I see what you're talking about! There's the street and our houses too!" Sherry squealed.

David rubbed his chin. "But…"

Sherry looked at her brother waiting for the end of the sentence. "But what David? Sherry asked him.

"There's only six houses on our street right?" Both Tina and Sherry nodded their heads.

"So, look at the map. There's another house that isn't here now," David said.

Tina was alarmed at the extra house on the map. "I'm twelve and I have never seen any other houses except the six that are here now."

Sherry was worried about Tina. She knew that Tina was a quiet sort of person and enjoyed the simple things in life. Sherry also knew that if the mystery continued much further, Tina would fall to pieces.

Tina was still a bit uneasy. She saw something else that the others hadn't. Something disturbing.

Chapter 18

The three stood by the boulder, gazing at the odd map. David and Sherry were excited about the new discovery, but Tina wasn't.

"Ya know David, you have taken a million pictures of me and Cody when we didn't want our pictures taken, but now that we could use your camera, you don't have it with you. Yeesh!" said Sherry.

"Look Tina! This has *got* to mean something! I mean, it has the tree, the boulder, all of the other trees and bushes out here. It even shows our street with more houses than there really is! Isn't this cool?" Sherry jumped up and down. Tina kept looking away from the etched map.

"Come on Tina. This might help us out a lot. Don't be so negative," said David.

Tina turned and faced David. "You think I'm being negative David? I'm not being negative at all, I'm frightened."

David looked confused and a bit angry. "Look Tina. Sherry and I are trying our best to help find our parents. Now I'm sorry if we're getting on your nerves or something, 'cuz we're not trying to. We're just worried, like you are."

Tina turned back around. "David I am so sorry for being so hard to get along with lately. It's just, I'm not used to this kind of stuff going on. Usually it's so quiet around here. Nothing bad ever happened. I just—can't." Tina fell apart. Tears ran down her face and dripped onto her purple shirt.

David felt bad for making her cry. He walked over and gave her a hug. "Okay Tina, I'm sorry for being so pushy. I'm not mad at you, believe me. Sherry and I are worried that if we don't figure this out soon, we'll never see any of our parents again. I'm really, really sorry," David said.

Tina wiped her face and sniffled. "I know I can't give up guys. I really do. I'm trying so hard not to fall apart but, it's getting difficult." She walked over to the boulder. She pointed to the area by the houses on the street. "This is why I am so upset. Look at that! There's something creepy above Mrs. Kings house. I don't know what it is, but I'm afraid that evil thing is going to hurt her or something," she said while trying not to fall apart again.

David and Sherry looked at the strange writing above Mrs. King's house. 'Βασίλισσα', it read. Sherry pulled a pen out of her pocket and drew the writing on her arm for reference.

"That's odd. I wonder what that means." said Sherry. "We should go back home and look it up on my computer. We need to check on Mrs. King and Cody anyway. He's probably eaten everything in the house by now." Sherry giggled.

David looked at his sister. "Oh *har-har!*" He turned to walk back home.

"I thought it was funny, didn't you Tina?" Sherry asked, not getting any response. "Okay, I'll shut up." Sherry said, stomping along the path home.

As they cleared the tree line, they noticed a person standing in the front window of the Franklin house.

"Hey, Mrs. Franklin is home now. Let's go talk to her first," David told the girls.

They headed straight for the elderly woman's home and knocked on the door. She slowly opened it, looking frightened and unsure. She steadied herself with a walker.

"Mrs. Franklin?" Tina asked.

"Yes?" the seemingly shy woman said to Tina.

"Hi, I'm Tina Brooks. I live on the other side of Mrs. King's house at the end of the street."

"I've seen you and the new family running about. I know who you are," the woman said back to Tina.

"Well, I was wondering—*we* were wondering if you had ever heard of anything odd happening around this area." Tina hoped for a bit of information that would help them.

"I remember when our son was young. He talked about hearing voices in the woods. But all grownups know that kids have wild imaginations. I didn't pay it any mind. He grew up and moved away years ago." The old woman looked saddened.

Tina elbowed Sherry. "Excuse me but, did you say he heard voices in the woods? Can I ask you what kind of voices?" Tina asked.

"Oh, you know how kids are. He used to go out and play in the woods for hours. Sometimes he didn't even

The Secret of Willow Patch

make it in for dinner. And he always had some grand story to tell Mr. Franklin and myself."

Tina became frustrated. "Mrs. Franklin, I don't mean to sound pushy or short, but it's very important for you to remember what your son heard exactly."

"It's been a *very* long time since our child was young. But let me see. Oh I remember now. He said that there was a talking tree in the woods. I remember laughing so hard about it. Imagine that! A talking tree!" the woman giggled at the memory.

The kid's eyes widened as they heard the words "talking tree". "Can you remember anything else ma'am? It's really important to us."

Tina tried to think of a reason for why something that was 'all in a child's mind' would be so important. "We're writing a report together at school about funny things that kids do and how they change as they grow up." Tina cracked a smile at David and Sherry.

"Oh, well, how interesting. Would you three like to come in and chat? It's been a very long time since I've had any company, and the stories I could tell you about our son Bobby! She motioned for them to come inside.

"Thank you very much Mrs. Franklin. You have a really nice home," Sherry commented.

"Would you all like something to drink? I don't have any soda pop, but I have some fresh tea." She offered the kids.

"No ma'am, but thank you for asking," Tina replied.

"So tell us about your son's stories. We'd like to get a really good grade on our report." Tina winked at David and Sherry.

The Beginning

"I remember a day when Bobby came in the house and was crying and telling his father and myself that he saw something glowing in the woods. I'll tell you, that boy was crying crocodile tears. He just wouldn't stop trying to convince me. It was a rough day. I remember having to ground him for a week because he seemed obsessed about this light he saw. It really worried me, but he eventually stopped talking about it." Mrs. Franklin pulled a tissue from a crochet covered box and dabbed the corner of her eye.

"I see, and did he say anything else after that?" Tina listened closely for any clues that would help them to figure out what was happening.

"No, that was pretty much the end of it for him. It seemed odd to me considering how much time he spent in there before, but it was better than him coming out of there with all those stories."

Tina glanced at a curio cabinet in the corner of the living room. On the top shelf was a sculpture of a very large tree. The tree that all the mystery came from. She eyeballed both David and Sherry and pointed it out to them silently.

"Mrs. Franklin, where did you buy that pretty tree sculpture?"

"Oh, let me take that out of the cabinet and show you. My son Bobby made that for me when he was about ten years old. Isn't it wonderful? It even has his signature on the bottom," she bragged.

"Wow! That really is nice Mrs. Franklin. Kind of reminds me of a really pretty picture of a tree that I recently drew."

Tina looked at Sherry and David with a raised brow.

"Yes, this is all I have left now."

Tina noticed the sculpture even had a carving on it, but it was too tiny to read.

"Well Mrs. Franklin, we need to get moving. We appreciate your time and the great story," Tina said as she walked toward the front door.

"Stop by any time kids. I don't get out much, due to my hip problems. It was nice talking to you all," the woman said as she waved while closing her door.

"Wow. That was weird," David commented. "Her son sculpted the tree? Man this tree really has a hold on this area."

"Yeah, and he heard the voices too, just like we did," Sherry added.

They walked faster back to David and Sherry's home. As they approached the front door, it swung open.

"Guys! Mrs. King is sick or something!" Cody screamed at them. Tina ran to Mrs. King's side. "Mrs. King? Mrs. King! Are you okay?" She didn't answer.

"Is she breathing?" David asked Tina. "Yes, but she won't wake up. Mrs. King!" Tina shouted, hoping to wake her.

"Okay, that's it! We *have* to call the police and an ambulance *now*. We can't handle all this alone anymore girls," David said.

Tina looked at Mrs. King's face and stood up in fear. "Oh my God! The boulder! Remember what I told you about that boulder and the weird marking above Mrs. King's house? I told you I was worried about her! Now that evil thing is probably killing her and it's all my fault for not doing what it told me to do! Our parents are never coming home!" Tina completely fell apart again.

Sherry whispered to David and she snuck upstairs to her bedroom. David tried to calm Tina as he glanced around for the cordless phone. He became aggravated knowing he needed to call the police, and more than likely, Cody had put the phone in some place that he would never find it.

Sherry immediately opened a browser on her computer and looked up the strange mark or writing that was above Mrs. King's house on the map.

"Dang it, I have to use a character map or something to look this up," she said, knowing that she couldn't use the English alphabet. She pulled up the character map and wasn't successful. None of the characters looked like what she drew on her arm earlier. She continued researching everything and anything to help out.

Tina sat by Mrs. King, brushing her hair away from her face. "You were always so nice to me," she said quietly to her old friend. "I'd give anything to make you better."

David searched all over the house for the cordless phone so he could call the police. "Cody! Where'd you put the phone?" David yelled to his little brother.

"I didn't put it anywhere!" Cody yelled back.

"Then where is it, Cody??" David got very impatient and panic stricken.

"David! Come here quick!" Sherry screeched down the stairs.

"What? What is it? You find the phone?" David yelled as he ran up the stairs, three steps at a time.

"Look at this! I went to a place called www.indentifymydrawing.com, and I drew an exact copy of the symbol or writing that was on that map. A guy there said that the symbol is Greek for the word 'queen'!" Sherry shouted excitedly.

David was stupefied. "You mean…?"

"*Yes*! Mrs. King must be the missing queen!" shouted Sherry.

David sat on the end of Sherry's bed. "You've gotta be kidding me. She's like—old, and I mean really old! Tina said she has lived on this street since she was really little."

Sherry rolled her eyes.

"David, I don't care how long she's been in that house. All I know is that *she* is the queen, and it's weird because her last name is King!" Sherry giggled.

"So—her name would be Queen King?" David covered his mouth trying not to laugh. "Seriously, that's just too funny." He stood up and went back downstairs. "Cody, have you found the phone yet?"

"No David! I don't know where it is!" Cody said in an annoyed voice.

David walked over to the couch where Mrs. King and Tina were. The old woman was still unconscious.

"Tina, can I talk to you for a second?" he asked his tearful friend. He guided her into the kitchen. "You are *not* going to believe this. Sherry is upstairs on her computer and she called me up to show me something incredible," David said, sounding like he held all the secrets of the universe.

"What is it David? I really need to stay with Mrs. King until an ambulance comes to get her. By the way, did you find the phone yet?" Tina asked, wiping tears off her face.

David paced back and forth nervously. "No, we haven't found the phone yet, but listen. The etching on the side of the boulder, the one that had the weird writing or whatever above Mrs. Kings house, it means 'queen' in the Greek language!" David said loudly.

Tina perked up a bit and then hung her head down again. "What good does that do us David? Poor Mrs. King isn't responding to anything I do or say. I'm really worried about her. Not just that but now that she is this sick, even if she *was* the queen, she can't walk there and we can't pick her up either." Tina sounded seriously depressed.

Sherry came down the stairs and joined Tina and David. "So what'd you think about the writing, Tina?" Sherry asked.

"If Mrs. King is the queen that the immortal or whatever it is wants, I don't know if I'd want to hand her over even if I could. She's always been so nice to me. If it *is* evil as I suspect it must be, I don't want any of us near it, let alone a sickly old woman. Besides, that would be just as bad as one of our parents feeding us to the wolves." Tina picked at her fingernails.

Sherry walked out to the living room. She looked at old Mrs. King. She thought to herself. "How could she be related to this thing that spoke to Tina? It must be the King that wants her back, but that would mean that Mrs. King is evil, too." Sherry tapped her foot as she watched the old woman breath lightly.

David and Tina walked in with long faces.

"Sherry, do you still have that fact sheet that you had earlier today?" asked Tina.

"No, it's over at your house, remember? I think I left it on your bed or something," Sherry replied.

"Okay, I'm going to go back over and get it and come right back. We need to update our fact sheet and work from there. You guys keep a really close eye on Mrs. King," Tina instructed them.

Tina entered her quiet home. She glanced in the kitchen where her mother loved cooking special meals for her and her father. She passed by the comfy chair that her dad sat in when he got home from work. It was very hard for Tina to be in her home without her parents, but she did in hopes of getting them back soon. She ran up the stairs to her bedroom.

"Okay, where's the pad of paper? Where's the list of facts Sherry made?" She looked all over her bed, the floor, just about everywhere in her room. Then she passed by her mirror and caught a glimpse of something different. She turned around like an actress in a scary movie, very slowly. There, in her mirror was the evil immortal. His face was horrifying as he glared at Tina with contempt. Tina jumped back away from the mirror.

"You now know who the queen is. Bring her to me now, or live your pathetic life without the ones you love!"

Chapter 19

Tina got angry. She loved Mrs. King like a grandparent and wanted to protect her, but she also wanted her parents back.

"That's not fair! You can't make me choose between a sweet old lady and my parents! Besides, Mrs. King, the queen, is sick. She can't even wake up let alone walk to the tree! What is it you want with her anyway?" Tina demanded to know.

"She belongs to me, young mortal one. You have no control over what is about to take place. You cannot stop it, and when it happens, you must bring her to me. If you do, I will free the adult humans. But don't try any tricks, I will be watching you," said the evil one. Then he faded away and Tina's mirror returned to normal.

"I can't believe that Mrs. King is his queen. She's too nice to be evil." Tina talked to herself trying to pull herself together and return to the Parker home.

"Is my babysitter going to Heaven soon?" asked little Cody.

David walked him into the kitchen. "Cody, she's sick. We aren't sure what's wrong with her and I might have to go to a neighbor's house to call for help since we can't find our phone." David tried not to upset his little brother but at the same time, he didn't want to lie to him.

"Hey David? Do you think she's going to be all right?" Sherry asked her brother.

"I don't know Sherry. She doesn't really seem to be in pain; she just isn't waking up." David helped her to understand.

Tina opened the door and walked in. "How's Mrs. King doing?" she asked David.

"Well no worse, but no better either. I think I'm going to go to Mrs. Franklin's house and call 911. We can't just leave her like this," he said.

"David, Sherry, I have some bad news." Tina tried to break the mirror experience to them easily. With all that has gone on since the Parkers moved in, either Sherry or David were liable to go off the deep end. "So, he knows that we know who the queen is, and if we don't take her to him, our parents are gone for good. But I can't get a grasp on how a sweet old woman like Mrs. King could be his queen. I mean, he was the meanest, creepiest thing I have ever seen. Pure evil." Tina shook her head, not wanting to believe that her best friend all these years lead a life of evil.

"That's really bizarre. And why would she be living a normal life like the rest of us here on this street if she's immortal? And if she is immortal, she wouldn't have aged. And why is her husband just now trying to get her back? He could've done this so many times when Tina was at that tree reading. Something just isn't adding up," said David.

"Yeah, this whole situation is making my skin crawl," said Sherry.

The Beginning

"I'm going down to the Franklin house to call 911 before we're all in trouble for not reporting our parents missing and now Mrs. King being in a coma," David said as he walked toward the front door.

"Don't David!" shouted Tina. David jumped as Tina yelled at him. He looked at her for an explanation. "The evil one said not to try and trick him and that he would be watching us." Tina shivered.

"So we can't do anything to help her? She could be dying as we speak!" David sounded more stressed than ever.

"I know David, but if we do anything other than what he says, we may lose our parents. I'm not saying that I'd rather lose Mrs. King, but what if she was an evil immortal? Are we willing to lose the lives of our parents for someone like that??" Tina glanced at Mrs. King, feeling horrible for even letting the thought into her mind. "No, it just can't be true. He must be wrong about her or something because she is just too nice of a person to do anything bad....*ever*!" Tina looked even more confused and upset.

David and Sherry suddenly had a look of shock on their faces. Their eyes fixated on something behind Tina.

"Tina my friend. You've always been such a good child," the voice said. Tina slowly turned around, facing the couch that Mrs. King laid on in a comatose state.

"Mrs. King?" Tina said in a shaky voice. "How? Why?" Tina was taken aback when she saw her well again.

"Tina, I don't have a lot of time to explain what is happening, but I will try to quickly. I am Queen Willow.

I chose to become human many years ago to learn the human way. Our people do not live the way you do. We are immortal, descendants of the original immortals of the world. My husband is King Willow and yes, he did live down the street when he was in human form. But he passed on long ago and was returned to his immortal life in Willow Patch as King, leaving me here, waiting to pass on as well so that I could rejoin him." The Queen tried to explain.

Tina, David, Sherry and Cody were all stunned. Their jaws hung down in complete awe of her Highness.

"So you and your husband chose to become humans?" Tina asked.

"Yes Tina. We ruled for a very long time in Willow Patch which is right below the woods you children play in. Many of the immortals wanted to be free to live above ground in the woods, but were afraid of human contact when houses were built so close. The king and I became human to see how humans would react to our kind. Unfortunately, the price of becoming human was not remembering who we really were until right before our bodies died," replied the Queen.

"But, begging your pardon Queen Willow, your husband the King was very mean and frightening when he spoke to me in the woods and again in my bedroom. He showed me wars among the good and evil immortals. He said that if I didn't return his queen to him, he would never release our parents." Tina said hesitantly.

"My husband would never say harsh words like that. He is a very good immortal, just like me. And he is as handsome as any being could possibly be. I truly believe that our goodness and love is what brought us back together in human form," said Queen Willow.

"Well he isn't nice now your highness. He referred to me as pathetic, and he wasn't even remotely handsome. The immortal I spoke with that said you 'belong to him' was a frightening sight." Tina said, trying not to be disrespectful.

"Tina, you said that the evil one referred to you as pathetic?"

"Yes ma'am," Tina replied quickly.

"Strailord! I should have known! He refers to all humans as pathetic. He must have come to Willow Patch to try to win my love." The Queen shed a tear while thinking of what could have become of her husband.

Tina cocked her head to one side. "Who is Strailord?"

The Queen shook her head in disgust. "Strailord is the Kings evil brother. He has always been jealous of the King and has vowed to make me his for many years. I thought he had finally given up, but it seems he still holds true to his broken character."

David decided to speak up. "Queen Willow, can I ask you a few questions?"

"Of course; if I can answer them I will," she said in reply.

"Okay, for one, why did all this strange stuff start happening right after our family moved here?"

"It was merely timing David, and no different than a leaf falling from a tree and landing on your head as you walk under it." She smiled.

"I can accept that as a valid answer. But what about the drawings? Tina drew a picture of the tree and it looked like someone had taken a picture of it. And it even happened when she drew something silly on my sister's computer. It wasn't even supposed to be a tree! Did Strailord make all that happen?" David felt he might stump her with his detective skills.

"My, you really do have a lot of questions don't you?" the Queen grinned at David. "Willow Patch is a very large community that is very close to all of your homes, and I suppose from time to time, they are able to contact you in ways that maybe you cannot understand. Even the evil immortals that manage to intrude on our peaceful city," she answered.

David wasn't sure what to think about her answer, but accepted it. "So the voices we have been hearing, before Strailord started talking to Tina, those were the voices of others like you?" he asked.

"David, our world is so unlike yours. Many humans have become cold to one another's needs, but we good immortals have always tried to help others as much as we can. We just haven't helped much outside of the woods because humans have changed so much. They stopped believing that there might be those that are different from them. So we moved our community below the woods, safe from humans that didn't want to try and understand who we were." She tried to answer David as best as she could.

"So, like everyone down there is magical? Because we had a little glowing thing heal us in the woods one night." David asked.

"Yes, there are those that are healers. Although in general, we do not show ourselves to humans, the healers are strongly attached to human suffering and will take a chance from time to time when needed," she answered David's question easily.

"Okay, that's cool." David nodded.

Sherry tugged on David's arm from behind him and whispered in his ear. "Ask her about when Tina was young and the tree lighting up."

"Oh yeah. Why did the tree light up when Tina went there the first time? Because she didn't even know that happened until the Strailord showed her." David inquired.

"The tree that you speak of is the entrance to Willow Patch. Up high on the trunk of the tree is where they exit and enter, from high above ground to below where Willow Patch is. Whenever anything magical gets near the tree, it lights up. But only the immortals that are down in Willow Patch can see the light. It serves as a protection device for our inhabitants. This way if anyone evil or good comes near the entrance, we know to be on alert or welcome them. Tina wouldn't have seen the light from above ground," she said as she smiled. All four of the kids looked stunned.

"But…..that would mean….," David said as he looked at Tina.

"That's right. Your friend, Tina is a descendant as well." Queen Willow clarified.

Tina sat down when she heard the shocking news. "But, that would mean my parents aren't really my parents." Tina looked sad.

"No child, they are in fact your biological parents. It is your grandparents on your mother's side that were immortals. They too, chose to become human and while in their human form, they had a child named 'Lilly'. When Lilly was older, she met your father in Middleton Heights High School. They weren't aware that your mother was a descendant either. But her music is her gift above Willow Patch. And your gift, Tina, is unconditional love. You have a very big heart, Tina. Big enough to love all those who feel unloved, and all those that aren't always nice to you, but still need love nonetheless. And when you and your mother pass on and return to Willow Patch as I will soon, your true powers will emerge," the Queen stated as she stood there still sporting old Mrs. King's body.

Tina looked at the Queen with tears in her eyes. "Thank you Ma'am. That was the best thing anyone has ever said to me."

The Queen became eerily silent and still. The children watched her as she appeared to be listening out for something that was coming.

"What's wrong with her?" little Cody asked David.

"Uh—I'm not quite sure Code man. It looks like she hears something," David tried to explain to Cody.

"Mrs. Ki...er—Queen Willow? Sherry tried to figure out why she looked the way she did, but received no reply. "Tina, what's going on with her?" Sherry asked her friend.

Tina stepped closer to the Queen and was confused by her condition. It was as if she was frozen solid, much like Tina herself was at the tree barrier.

"Your Highness? Are you okay?"

David started to back up from the queen. "Oh no. We've already done this once before with Tina. Mr. Creepfest must be talking to her and I don't want anything to do with him!" David exclaimed. Cody darted behind his big brother for protection from the evil being he spoke of. "Cody, go upstairs—*now!*" David yelled.

Cody ran across the room and up the stairs as fast as he could. His bedroom door slammed hard and was heard by everyone downstairs, except the Queen.

As if suspended in time, Queen Willow stood in the Parker living room. They all worked at getting the Queen to recover from her motionless state, but nothing worked.

"Well Tina, what do you suppose we do now?" David asked.

Tina touched Queen Willow's arm. "Is this what I looked like at the tree?"

"*Yes!*" David bellowed back her.

"Tina jumped. "Dang it David! That was just what I needed, someone to scare the heck out of me when I'm already afraid!" Tina screamed in David's ear. David looked mortified.

"Sorry Tina. This whole thing is getting to be too much. I guess I snapped a bit."

"Ya think?" answered Tina. "Do you honestly think I am enjoying this? Cuz I'm not! My nerves are a mess David and all I can do is worry about our parents," Tina added.

The Queen stood there like a statue, her eyes were glazed over. Suddenly Tina saw a movement in the Queen's hand.

"I wish Mom and Dad were here," said Sherry staring at the Queen.

"Shhh!" said Tina as she watched the Queen slowly begin to move again.

"No, no, no..." the Queen uttered as she began to move and realize what was happening.

"You're back," said Tina as she watched Queen Willow re-animate.

The Queen looked horrified as she came to. "My husband — the King — it can't be!"

The kids tried to make sense of what she was saying. Queen Willow fell to the floor in tears. The body she had lived in for sixty-four years was shuttering. Tina dropped to her knees on the floor next to the Queen.

"Queen Willow, what is it? What's wrong?" Tina asked.

Tina knew that it had to be bad news by the look on the Queens face and the shake in her voice.

"Tina, the King has been cast upon by Strailord and is in a sleep state, unable to wake."

Tina was speechless for a moment, in order to gather her thoughts. "I'm so sorry Queen Willow. Is there anything we can do to help you or the King?"

Queen Willow shed tears for her beloved King, knowing that there was only one way to help him. She had to be there in Willow Patch, which seemed easy enough for an immortal, but the process was something that most humans cannot comprehend. The Queen wiped the tears from her elderly human face. "Tina, can I speak with you alone for a moment?" Sherry tugged on David and Cody's arms and led them out of the room.

"Tina my friend, in my human form, you were the very thing that kept my body and mind going after my husband passed on and went back to Willow Patch. If it hadn't been for your friendship through the years, I would have felt the pain of being apart from my husband all the more." The Queen emphasized.

Tina looked at the Queen with honor. "Queen Willow, I loved the times we spent together feeding your Hummingbirds and planting flowers in your garden. I wouldn't change a thing, I hope you know that," Tina replied as she bowed her head slightly, to assure the Queen that she wasn't upset about being a part of her life. "In fact, I treasure those times," Tina said with a big smile.

Queen Willow knew that Tina was the one person who would understand and help her without any hesitation. "I am quite positive that you are a pure soul Tina. Your goodness radiates from you and I know that with your help, I will soon be reunited with my beloved. There is however, something I have to tell you and you must promise me you will not stray from what you must do. It will be difficult, but always remember there is a good purpose behind it."

Tina looked at the Queen. She felt the truth as she spoke as if it were waves of water running across her soul and mind. Tina trusted the Queen with her very life.

The Queen continued. "Now child, just as my husband passed on in his human form and returned to Willow Patch, so must I." She smiled at Tina hoping she could comprehend what must happen soon.

"So, you're going to die?" Tina asked to clarify the horrifying words that came from The Queens mouth.

"Yes child, but I will go back home to Willow Patch. Don't fret Tina. Death is a very natural part of life, just as birth. But there is one difference with people who were once immortals".

Tina cocked her head to the side, trying to figure out the difference. Queen Willow described the process to Tina.

"Tina, because we are a magical type of being, certain words need to be spoken as the human form dies. Much like the last words that are said when normal humans pass on."

Tina understood the Queen and was ready to do whatever she needed, even if it meant the death of her old friend, Mrs. King.

"When is this going to happen? And how will we ever get our parents back without your help here? None of the other adults around here help us at all."

"My dear, the time is at hand, and do not fear your situation with your parents. I may leave you as a human, but I will be with you in my immortal form." The Queen winked at Tina.

"But, I don't understand. You said that when this body dies, you go back home to Willow Patch. How can you be with me if you're there and I'm here?" Tina was trying so hard to make sense of it all.

The Queen looked as if she was getting weak. "Call your friends back so we may go to the tree and end my long journey here," the Queen said.

Tina yelled out to her friends. "Come on guys, we have something to do."

David, Sherry and Cody entered the living room and saw the Queen looking as if she was ready to fall over.

"What's going on Tina?" Sherry asked.

"We need to take the Queen to the tree now," Tina said with deep regret in her voice.

David's left eyebrow raised a bit. "We have to go back out there again?"

"Yes David, now," Tina said.

"But she doesn't look like she's in any shape to walk to the tree," Sherry said, glancing at the Queen.

"I will be fine, but we must go now children," the Queen said.

As they left the Parker house, Tina saw that all the neighbors once again had their curtains opened. The elderly occupants stood in their windows and watched as the children escorted the old woman into the woods.

"Uhm, Queen Willow—the people are all watching us again," David said.

The Queen glanced over her shoulder. "Never you mind, David," she said, forging ahead as if nothing out of the ordinary was happening. The sun was low in the sky and the dark was quickly approaching. The Queen appeared to be weakening more with each step. Tina and David held onto her arms, assuring she didn't collapse.

"Almost—there," Queen Willow uttered quietly.

They saw the tree up ahead, and the closer they got to the tree, the more Tina's stomach turned. Finally they arrived and the Queen laid her hands upon the tree as she slowly slid down and fell over.

"Queen Willow!" Tina squealed in horror.

"It is time now Tina. This human body cannot hold out much longer. You must take this parchment that I have kept for years, and you must read the words before it is too late."

The Queen's breathing was short and labored. Tina took the parchment with the words from the Queens shaking hand. She felt the parchment and could tell it had been around for a very long time. Sorrow fell upon Tina as she began to read the words, but she continued as instructed. David, Sherry and Cody all stood by and watched.

> You lived a life in human form,
> But now you must return once more,
> To Willow Patch where you belong,
> A human you must bring along.

Chapter 20

The Queens old body stopped breathing right as Tina realized what she had said. She turned to her friends with a look of shock in her eyes as she faded away, along with the body that the Queen had resided in.

"Where did Tina go?" yelled David. He ran over to where the Queen and Tina were just moments before, and was stunned. "They're gone!" David was frantic.

Sherry began to cry uncontrollably while holding her little brother Cody. "Why did Tina go with the Queen?" Sherry asked David as he ran his hands across the ground where it happened.

"I don't think she had a choice Sherry. You heard what she read from the parchment—'a human you must bring along'. I guess the Queen chose Tina to bring with her." David shook his head trying to figure out how to get Tina back. "This is great! This is just unbelievably *great*!" David said sarcastically. He looked up at the tree as the sun disappeared completely.

"You scare us all! You take our parents, and *now* you take Tina to get your Queen back???" David kicked at the tree in anger. "You may be big cool immortals in there, but to me, you're just a bunch of jerks!"

David slammed down onto the ground and shed a tear for the loss of his friend Tina.

Sherry walked over to David and sat down beside him. "I'm sorry David. She was my friend too and I'm going to miss her so much," said Sherry trying to comfort her brother's obvious broken heart. Sherry always figured that David had a bit of a crush on Tina, but she tried to be cool and not say anything about it.

"So what are we supposed to do now Sherry?" asked David.

"I don't know, but we can't just give up. Remember when Tina was so upset and she seemed like she wanted to give up?"

"Yeah I remember," he replied.

"Well we told her we couldn't give up and just because she's gone now, doesn't mean we can give up. It means we have to try even harder to fix this," Sherry said, sounding optimistic.

David looked impressed with his kid sister's demeanor, considering all that has happened.

"You're right. I mean, what do we honestly have to lose now? Everyone that meant anything to us is gone. We might as well do anything we can to figure this out. The only thing that I worry about at this point is Strailord. The only immortal that *was* here to deal with him if he attacked us, or something, is gone. It's just us now."

David, Sherry, and Cody all sat at the tree and watched as the last bit of daylight faded away while they brainstormed.

"Okay, the only thing I can think of right now is to go back to all the neighbors houses and talk to them again. I mean, I know we didn't get very far with any of them the last time, but it's all we have to go on right now. Besides, pretty soon it'll be too late to go knocking on their doors and visiting. You thought they were cranky earlier, imagine how bad they'd be if three kids came over and woke them when they've gone to sleep for the night!" David joked.

Sherry and Cody chuckled at the thought as they all started walking out of the woods. They decided to go to Mr. Pendleton's house first.

"Let's try to be as nice as possible, even though he is an old grump," Sherry said to her brothers.

"Yeah, but don't tell him about our parents being gone, too, or he'll get the police involved, and you know what Strailord told Tina about being tricky," David said.

They knocked at his door. The front porch light came on and the door opened. The old man stood there as if some hideous monster was standing right behind him.

"Are you okay Mr. Pendleton?" David asked.

"One—two—three," the old man whispered.

Sherry looked at David with a partial grin.

"Where's the other girl? Last time you came here, there was another girl—the one that was asking most of the questions and this little one wasn't with ya," Mr. Pendleton demanded to know.

"You mean Tina?" replied Sherry.

"She disappeared with the Queen," Cody responded rather quickly.

David was ill at ease with Cody's answer.

"What? She disappeared with the Queen you say?" the old man inquired. He opened his door further.

Sherry could see that he had been hopelessly alone for a very long time. The house was in a chaotic state. She thought about how clean her mother always kept their home.

"Mr. Pendleton, could we please come in and talk?" asked David.

Mr. Pendleton took a step back and allowed them to come in. They all looked for a place to sit down as he picked up assorted newspapers and clothing that was scattered on the furniture.

"Now tell me about this girl—Tina, how did she disappear? You're not here to harass me are ya? 'Cuz I'll toss the three of ya out on your backsides if ya are!" the old man said in a grouchy tone.

"No, Mr. Pendleton, please. We aren't here to harass you or make fun of you. We're here to get help or maybe, some information." Sherry said to the man as he took a seat on an old wooden stool.

"Well I suppose I can tell ya what I know or at least what I've seen—in *those* woods. It was a long time ago, 1982—back when the Mrs. and I were still married.

"I was out huntin' one evening like I did a lot back then. My wife loved venison; that's deer meat if ya don't know. I always knew where the best spots were to find them deer. I carried sticks with fluorescent tape on top so I could find the places where the best huntin' was for the next time I went out."

David stared at Sherry to get her attention. His mouth said the word "stick" to Sherry without the voice. Sherry nodded at David.

Mr. Pendleton continued "I was walkin' around right before the sun went down and I heard some talkin'. I wasn't used to hearin' nobody talkin' out that far, so I went lookin' to see who it was. Now I wish I wasn't so dern nosey."

David walked over to where the old man was sitting. "What did you see Mr. Pendleton?" David asked him.

The old man looked as if he was watching a replay of it in his mind. He looked terrified. "I stopped when I got close enough to the voices to hear them real clear. I peeked around the tree and saw them. It was Mr. King from down the road a bit, and he had that Franklin kid with him," he said as he shook his head.

"What were they doing?" Sherry asked.

Mr. Pendleton stood up from his wooden stool and paced. "It was like some sort of witch spell or something. The craziest thing I have ever seen. There laid Mr. King on the ground by a big old tree and the Franklin kid was saying somethin' that sounded like a poem as he stood over him. Next thing I knew, they were both gone. They just vanished. Now I don't want none of you kids tellin' people around here about this, 'cuz if ya do, I'll deny it — I will." The old man exclaimed.

"Oh we won't Mr. Pendleton, we promise. But what you just told us about: can I ask you just one question about it?" David implored.

The man nodded his head.

"We were at Mrs. Franklin's house earlier today and she made it sound like her son Bobby was still alive. As a matter of fact she never told us that he died or disappeared." David told the old man.

"Well I'm thinkin' that if you had a ten-year-old son never come home from the woods, you'd be a bit off yer rocker as well. Then her husband up and died and left her alone with all of her nightmares to live with until she kicks the bucket. I'm surprised the woman has made it this long!" he told the children in a 'matter of fact' way.

Sherry and David exchanged glances.

"Poor Mrs. Franklin. She seemed like such a nice lady," said Sherry.

"She still is!" David exclaimed. "Geez Sherry, she's still the same person, she just had a bad experience."

Sherry hung her head in embarrassment.

"You kids should stay clear of them woods. Not many people around here know the woods like me. I spent a lot of years out there hunting. Most folks would get lost out there easily," he warned the kids.

David started walking to the front door. "Well Mr. Pendleton, we appreciate your honesty."

Sherry and Cody followed their brother out the door and into the dark.

"Okay, well now we know this has happened before. No wonder he was watching us so much. He was probably just worried about us," David stated.

Sherry held Cody's hand as they walked to Mrs. Franklin's home. They knocked on the door, hoping she wasn't asleep. The elderly woman spoke through the door.

"Who is it? Who's out there?" Mrs. Franklin sounded terrified to open the door.

David looked up at her porch light and noticed the bulb was missing.

"Mrs. Franklin, it's me David Parker. We need to talk to you again if it's not too late."

The door opened just a bit for the woman to peek through. Once she saw the kids, she opened it all the way.

"Thank you Mrs. Franklin. I'm sorry it's late, but we need to talk to you about something really important," David said to her.

Mrs. Franklin invited them in. They sat down on her couch and readied themselves for an uncomfortable talk.

"So what can I do for you kids this evening? Do your parents know you're outside this late?" the old woman asked.

Sherry elbowed David and whispered in his ear. "Let me field this one David." He gave her the okay and Sherry started her very difficult conversation with the nice woman.

"Yes, Mrs. Franklin, our parents know we're out. They trust us enough." Sherry made up whatever she could to make her believe what she was saying.

"I never let my Bobby out after dark. No way. Wild animals you know," Mrs. Franklin whispered as she adjusted her sore legs.

"Yes, I know about the wild animals Mrs. Franklin, we're careful at ni...."

The old woman interrupted Sherry. "Those woods. They're not safe at night or even in daylight. They can be very deceiving you know. Oh how Bobby would play in those trees out there. For hours and hours—sometimes

191

days and days." She glanced at the tree sculpture that her son had made for her long ago.

David spoke up with concern. "Days and days? Mrs. Franklin, your son Bobby played for days before he would come home?"

She looked at the old cuckoo clock hanging on her wall. "He should be home anytime now. He loves company! We could all jump up and say surprise when walks through the door. My Bobby loves surprises!"

Sherry and David looked confused and horrified all at once. "Uhm, Sherry—yeah, I think we need to get moving." David realized just how badly the disappearance of Bobby had affected the poor woman.

"Oh don't leave! Bobby would love to have some new friends to play with!"

It broke the kid's hearts to have to walk away from poor Mrs. Franklin. She was so sad and so lost without her son and husband for so long.

Cody was tired and dragging his feet as they walked to the Talbot house where King Willow was raised. "Okay guys, one more house and hopefully we'll be able to make some sense of all this. Cody, hang in there dude. We'll go home soon and you can eat and get some sleep, I promise," said David.

They approached Mrs. Talbot's home, remembering how she slammed the door in their faces earlier that day.

Sherry knocked lightly, not wanting to frighten her at night.

"Coming!" they heard her yell from inside the house. The door opened.

"Do you kids realize what time it is?" she snipped at them.

"Yes ma'am, we do. Our parents gave us permission to come talk to you." David said loudly.

"What on earth do you kids need with me at this hour? You should all be in bed!" she bellowed at them.

"Look Mrs. Talbot, we need to come in and talk with you if you don't mind. It's kind of buggy out here," Sherry said using bug bites as an excuse to gain entrance into Mrs. Talbot's home.

Mrs. Talbot watched as mosquitoes and gnats landed on the kids arms and legs and decided to allow them into her home.

"Okay, sit down and tell me what is so important that you have to bother an old woman late at night." She was not happy they were there bothering her, but came to accept it as they talked.

They walked into the pristine living room and took seats on the antique coach. Mrs. Talbot looked them over as she sat down in her rocker.

David started the conversation. "Mrs. Talbot, we really appreciate this because we have spoken to the other neighbors around here and wanted to speak to you, too."

Mrs. Talbot picked up her knitting needles and began to knit as she listened to them. She mumbled to herself. "Knit one, pearl two, that's all I have left to do."

Sherry and David looked at each other.

Sherry whispered to him. "Is this one cuckoo too??"

David cracked an impish grin and continued to try to get through to the eighty-four-year old woman. "Mrs. Talbot, you've lived here most of your life right?"

She gave him a quick glance. "Yep. At least the good years when my husband and my son were still alive."

"What was your son's name—if you don't mind me asking," David inquired.

She pointed to a picture on her wall. "That's my son. We named him Eddie the day he came to us," she replied, as she continued her knitting.

"I'm sorry, but did you say he came to you?" Sherry asked the fragile woman.

"Yes, it was so peculiar. One day my husband Henry and I were in our yard pruning the rose bushes, when out of the woods walked these two children, a young boy and a girl. We knew everyone on the street and knew that they didn't live here, and they wore assorted foliage around them, like they had sprouted out from the ground."

Mrs. Talbot put her knitting needles down and walked over to the picture of her son on the wall.

"We always hoped to have a son, but the doctor told me I was barren and would never have children unless we adopted. It broke my heart as well as Henry's. We knew we couldn't afford to adopt, so when these children walked out of the woods, we saw it as a gift," she said, as she straightened the picture of Henry.

"So, what happened to the little girl Mrs. Talbot?" Sherry asked.

"The Curtis' next door took her in. They had two boys and wanted a little girl so badly."

Sherry nodded.

The old woman continued her story. "Eddie was such a good boy. He was the pride of his father and myself. But he grew up too fast and strangely enough, began to fancy the girl he walked out of the woods with. He was only sixteen when they started going out to the woods for walks. Before we knew it, Eddie was thirty years old and had asked her to marry him." A tear ran down her face as she spoke of her son.

"That's really cool Mrs. Talbot. I mean, that the same two kids that walked out of the woods together ended up getting married," David said.

She turned and walked back to her chair.

"What was her name Mrs. Talbot? The girl he married," David asked her.

"Oh, the Curtis' named her Olivia. That was Mrs. Curtis' favorite name," she said, staring at her son's picture from across the room. "It was a shame though. The Curtis' died in a car accident in—I believe it was 1975. Olivia was twenty-nine then and so beautiful. I suppose I can see why my son married her. She was a wonderful girl; lots of zest for life.

"After they married, they moved into her home since her parents had passed away."

David, Sherry and Cody all listened for any clues that might help them.

"Mrs. Talbot, can I ask you why, when they got married, their last name was King instead of Talbot?"

The frail woman's head hung as she answered David.

"Yes, that was an odd situation. When Eddie turned eighteen, he came to us and said he wanted to legally change his surname to King. He said that he had always known his last name, but he didn't mind using ours while we raised him. So he went to town and had his name changed. I can't say that it didn't bother me somewhat, but he was an adult then and I didn't want to cause a fuss with him. I loved him too much to hurt his feelings."

Sherry stood up. "So that's why Mrs. King had that name instead of Talbot! This whole place is like an unsolved puzzle that was waiting for us to move in."

David yanked Sherry back down onto the couch.

"Thanks for stating the obvious again Sherry," David replied to her in a snotty tone. Cody giggled.

"One more question and then I promise we'll leave," said David. "When we went to Mrs. Franklin's house to talk to her, she was acting like her son Bobby was still around, but Mr. Pendleton said that her son Bobby disappeared in the woods one day. Do you have any idea why she is acting that way?"

Mrs. Talbot stood up from her chair and pointed at David. "I can tell you this much boy, she isn't and never was crazy. Her son did in fact disappear in the woods." She coughed a bit, sounding very distressed. "I know because he was with my son Eddie when he went missing. Olivia was at home when Eddie said he wanted to go gather some flowers for her. He left the house and never came home again. Olivia was heartbroken. She never remarried either. She stayed in that same house all these years.

"But she doesn't stay inside all the time like the rest of us mind you. When her husband disappeared, she went through a short mourning and was right back to doing what she loved, taking care of those Hummingbirds," she said sounding angry. "The rest of us on this street just stay inside our homes. Those woods are dangerous, and being this close to them, we just as soon wait to die in our homes than to venture outside and disappear like my son and little Bobby Franklin."

David could see her point and nodded. "I can just imagine how scared you and the other neighbors must have been. Did anyone contact the police or go out and search for them?" David asked curiously.

"Of course we did, Child! When people turn up missing, you don't just sit around and do nothing! There were police out there for days, but they never found so much as a hint of either one of them."

David could see that she had answered enough questions and motioned to Sherry and Cody to get up. "Mrs. Talbot, thank you for all the information. I know you're very tired, so we'll get moving on home." David said as they all left the old woman's home.

Chapter 21

"Okay guys, time to go back home and let Cody get some sleep, and Sherry, you and I have *got* to brainstorm," David said in a commanding tone.

"Yeah, I'm really tired, but I miss Mom and Dad so much," said little Cody as he tried to keep his feet moving.

"We all do Cody. But we'll find them, I promise," Sherry said to her tired little brother.

They entered the dark silence of the Parker home. David started turning lights on. "Okay Cody, run upstairs and pile into bed. You look like a zombie," David joked with his brother. Cody slowly walked up the stairs and went to bed.

"Wow, I'm surprised he didn't ask for something to eat before he went to bed!" Sherry said with a chuckle.

"Poor kid is worn out Sherry, and I am too, but we have to keep working on this," David said to Sherry.

They walked into the kitchen for a few drinks and sat at the table. "Man it feels weird in here with Mom and Dad gone," David observed.

"Yeah, it's eerie," Sherry said as she looked around the kitchen. "I can't stop thinking about what old lady

Talbot said. She seemed so sad. And now we know Mrs. King's first name was Olivia, and the King was Eddie."

David looked at Sherry over his glass of milk. "King Eddie? I'm pretty sure his first name in Willow Patch was something more powerful sounding than Eddie," he said.

Sherry tapped her fingernails on her glass. "I wonder what their real first names are." Sherry searched her mind for cool sounding King and Queen names. "King Randolph Willow!" she shouted out.

David became annoyed. "Sherry! I don't care if their names are Queen Fifi and King Beau! I just want to get our parents and the Brooks family back! Now be serious for a while, will ya?" David was at the end of his 'patience' rope and was having major problems trying to stay focused. He was tired and knew that considering the ages of the neighbors, there wasn't any chance of getting help from them.

"Sorry David, I didn't mean to make you mad. I was just…"

"Look, Sis, don't worry about it. You didn't deserve to get your head bitten off. I'm just so confused and worried and I have no clue what to do," David said with tears in his eyes.

Sherry wasn't used to seeing that side of her brother. "David look, we aren't going to be able to do anything tonight anyway. Cody is asleep and we can't leave him alone. Besides its so dark out, we'd just end up getting lost out there again." She stood up from the kitchen chair and put her glass in the sink. "We might as well get some sleep, too, and tomorrow we can try again, okay?"

David put his glass in the sink. "Ya know, if Mom was here, these glasses would be washed in five seconds," he said with a slight giggle.

"Yeah, she's great isn't she?" Sherry replied. "I guess you're right, though. We'd probably end up lost, then we'd be no help to them at all."

David walked out of the kitchen and headed for the stairwell. He glanced at the clock as he passed it, thinking how his parents would never let him be awake that late at night.

Sherry and David checked on Cody and saw that he was fast asleep.

"Maybe we should just crash in here with Cody since Mom and Dad aren't here," David suggested.

Sherry nodded and went to get her pillow and blanket from her bed. They crashed on the floor of Cody's bedroom and were soon fast asleep.

At 8:00A.M. the next morning, a knock was heard at the door. David, Sherry and Cody all woke up thinking it was their parents.

"Mom! Dad!" They all shrieked as they heard the knocking. They ran down the stairs as fast as they could. David flew through the living room and opened the front door. To his dismay, it wasn't his parents.

"Is this the Parker home?" A policeman inquired.

David was shaking all over, as was his sister and brother. "Yes sir," David replied. David looked in the driveway and saw the official Middleton Heights police car.

"Can I speak to one of your parents?" the officer asked.

David panicked, and tried hard to come up with a viable story.

"They're—out jogging. Yeah, they do that every morning."

"I see, and can I ask you kids why you weren't in school yesterday?"

Sherry was feeling sick and didn't want to talk. Policemen always made her a bit nervous. Luckily enough, her brother didn't have the same fear and dealt with the officer himself.

"We all had fevers yesterday morning, so Mom kept us home," David responded.

Sherry coughed a few times to make the story seem more real to the officer.

David continued his excuse. "And since we just moved here, our phone doesn't work yet, so Mom was just going to send us back when we were better, with notes," David replied, hoping he would believe him.

The officer looked over the children into the house. "When do you think your parents will be back?" he asked them.

"We never know. Sometimes they get lost out in those woods while they're jogging and it takes them longer to get home. Sir, if you don't mind, we really need to get back in bed before our parents get back and see us out of bed. Mom made us promise that we'd stay in bed while they were gone." David tried one more time to get the officer to go away, knowing that Strailord told Tina not to try any tricks on him.

"Okay look you kids, if you have any problems before your folks get home, go to one of your neighbor's homes and use the phone to call 911, okay?" he said sounding concerned.

"Yes sir, I will. I'm almost thirteen so my mom figured I could babysit my brother and sister alone for a while. And we've already met all the neighbors, so we will be fine," David said as he closed the door.

David's face looked pale as if he really was sick after talking to the police officer. "Dang it, I never expected the school to send the police out here," David mumbled.

"David, what if he comes back before we find Mom and Dad? Will he take us away and put us in some orphanage or something?" Sherry asked her brother.

David hugged his sister and brother. "Nobody is taking us anywhere guys. We're going to find Mom and Dad today, I promise you that. Now let's go get something for breakfast before we start out today. We can plan what we're going to do at the table."

They headed for the kitchen. Cody sat at the table while Sherry and David pulled out boxes of cereal and milk.

"Cody, what kind of cereal do you want this morning?" Sherry asked.

"I don't know. Mom usually gets it for me."

Cody was not doing well with his parents being gone for so long.

"Okay, well we have four different kinds, so just point to one and I'll pour it for you." Sherry said feeling like she had become a "fill in" mother.

Cody pointed to the box with the fruity rings. Sherry poured it in the bowl and covered it with milk.

"You're going to have to come with us today Code," David said. "We'll bring a backpack with some granola bars and juice boxes with so we don't have to keep coming back home."

"No kidding. I don't want to have to pick raspberries all day!" Sherry said loudly.

"Okay, Sherry, so let's figure out where we need to go, judging by all of the clues and everything that has happened the past few days. We know it all started with us going to that tree. That's where we started hearing the whispering. Then the pictures that Tina drew. Cody and I saw the carving in the tree, but you and Tina didn't see them.

"Oh, and when we were lost in the woods, that glowing thing landed on your shoulder and it healed us. Then Dad and Mr. Brooks found us, but when we got home, both our moms were gone. Our dads went missing and Tina started getting messages from Strailord. Oh, and let's not forget that it turned out Mrs. King was in fact the immortal Queen Willow!" David summarized.

Sherry ate her cereal while thinking of everything that had happened.

David pushed the cereal around in his bowl. "I can't even eat knowing that Mom and Dad are missing along with the whole Brooks family."

"David, you have to eat. We'll find them or figure out something, but if you give up, we're sunk and so is everyone else," Sherry said in a demanding voice.

"Is Mommy stuck in that tree still?" asked little Cody.

"We don't know Code. All we know is the picture on my computer showed Mom and Mrs. Brooks under the roots," Sherry stated.

"Maybe the tree got Daddy too," Cody said with his mouth full of cereal.

"We really don't know, but let's hope that wherever they are, they're all safe," David said on a chipper note.

They finished up their breakfast and began to pack up David's large backpack with food and drink to last for most of the day. "Okay guys, let's go back out to that blasted tree and see if we can find a way in or something. Remember, the Queen said that the tree was the entrance and exit of Willow Patch," David said.

"Yeah but she said the entrance was high above the ground. We can't climb that thing, it's *huge!*" Sherry exclaimed.

David stopped walking for a moment and looked at Sherry. "Yeah *and* people don't live underground, and tree's don't talk either!" David's tirade was short lived but effective. Sherry shrugged her shoulders and kept walking.

As they approached the tree that was once a fun place, they began to feel stressed.

"It's still pretty, but knowing that Mom and Mrs. Brooks are probably stuck in there, I keep getting creeped out." Sherry uttered.

David slowly walked toward the roots, knowing that was where the invisible barrier was. He reached his hand out slowly, all the while remembering what happened to Tina when she touched the barrier. David's hands stretched out further and further with nothing to stop him.

"Sherry, uhm—it's gone," David said to his sister as he felt around the roots for the area where the barrier once was.

The Beginning

He climbed up under the roots, just like all the kids did the day they he and Cody first saw it. "I can't believe this! It's gone and so are Mom and Tina's mom too! They were right here! The picture showed them right in this very spot!"

David became louder and louder, his feet kicking around at the dirt below the roots. "Okay!" David yelled up to the tree. "We've had enough! You took our parents, you took Tina's parents *and* Tina, and you even got your Queen back! What more do you want?" David screamed at the top of his lungs.

Sherry and Cody climbed under the roots to comfort and calm their brother. "David, calm down. Getting mad like that won't help. Believe me, I'm the queen of blowing up. It never helped me out before either." Sherry tried to soothe her brother's rage at the tree.

They all sat together under the huge roots, hoping for a miracle. A memory or something that would just click and make them realize what they needed to do.

David fell to pieces. He picked up a twig that was under the cover of the roots and snapped it in two. "No! You can't just keep them all! That's not fair! We're all alone now! We need help. We need Tina back to figure this out." He covered his face to hide his tears.

Sherry spoke up. "Please—please help us to understand what is going on. We're just human beings,"

Suddenly their answer came. "Swear your silence."

David jumped up and smacked his head on the tree. "What the heck?" he yelled at the tree. "Swear our silence? About what? About all of our parents being abducted by a tree? Is that what you want us to swear our silence about? I don't think you have anything to worry about, because if we told anyone other than people that live out here about a talking tree, they'd have us all slammed in a rubber room!"

"Swear your silence!" the voice said louder to the kids.

Sherry became frightened. "David, please don't anger it," she said quietly to her enraged brother.

"I'm scared Sherry!" Cody said as he cried and crawled behind his sister.

"Come on! Answer me! Why do we have to swear our silence? Huh? Maybe I'll go tell the police, or better yet the President!" David was out of control.

"David, stop!" Sherry begged him. "You're scaring Cody and yelling at the tree isn't helping the situation at all," Sherry tried once more to reason with him. Sherry finished her sentence and got up to take Cody home, but as quickly as she got up, the barrier came down. Sherry slammed into the invisible wall.

"No!!!!" The kids all yelled as they realized they were now prisoners of the tree just as their mother, Mrs. Brooks and more than likely, both of their fathers were.

Outside, the tree looked beautiful as always. Birds enjoyed the ample branches and leaves. Silence filled the air and the sky was baby blue, spotted with fluffy clouds here and there. It was, in fact, another beautiful day in the woods that beckoned to all who were near.

The End